THE SEVEN TOWERS
OF
TRINKOLAI

AND OTHER TALES
OF
FANTASY AND WONDER

Mark McCabe

First published 2022 by
Serotine Press Australia
PO Box 193
Nambucca Heads NSW 2448
Australia
www.serotinepress.com.au
publishing@serotineinc.com

Cover design, layout and editing by
Serotine Editing and Publishing Services
www.serotine.com.au

Cover image from istockphoto.com

ISBN: 978-0-6486768-3-6

A catalogue record for this book is available from the National Library of Australia

FOR

JOSH

AND

RYAN

CONTENTS

TIME TO REFLECT

In Verinor, beside the old road that leads from Kadrine to Syrpan, lies a small and quite unassuming cottage. It is just a shell now, abandoned and at the mercy of the elements. With no-one to hinder their passage, a host of vines and climbing shrubs have clambered up and over its walls, gaining entrance wherever an opening permits. The pale blue colour which had once adorned its exterior is now all but gone — faded away or hidden behind those verdant intruders. Thistles and all manner of other weeds reign supreme in the surrounding garden. Not a flower can be seen.

But it was not always like this. Lorelei lived there for a while. At that time, its beauty was almost a match for hers.

It was in those days, while Nicolas I sat upon the Amethyst Throne, that Kova chanced to see her one day as he was passing by. His eyes had been drawn to her cottage as soon as he had rounded the bend in the road and first caught sight of it. The sky-blue walls with white trim around the windows, all surmounted by a covering of fresh, golden thatch, were what first drew his attention. He was on foot, and thus had time as he approached to take in the rest of its features.

As his gaze shifted to the colourful garden which surrounded the dwelling, he began to see that, if anything, it only served to further enhance the building's charm, much as the intricately carved form of a brooch or ring might provide the perfect setting in which to display a precious gem. The surrounding acre or so of grounds was a mass of varying hues, with flowers and shrubs of every kind, each perfectly placed, its own beauty enhancing that of its neighbour while at the same time justifying its own place in the overall tableau. If the leaves of a few of the trees which dotted the surrounding space hadn't been swaying gently in the breeze, he could easily have thought he was looking at a painting rather than a real home.

With his mind filled with such pleasant considerations, Kova received quite a start when, just as he was about to pass the front gate, a young woman suddenly stood up from amongst a gaggle of shrubs and greeted him, gracing him as she did so with a broad smile that lit up the whole of her face.

To Kova, this surprising apparition was even more stunning than the house and its surrounds. She was, quite simply, one of the most beautiful young women he had ever set eyes on. For a few moments, he just stood there, gaping back at her, his thoughts in turmoil as a host of unexpected emotions coursed through him in quick succession.

"Hello," he eventually managed to respond. "What are you doing?"

"Oh, just tending our garden. It tends to run riot at this time of the year if we don't keep at it." She paused then, looking down intently at what she had been working on for a few moments before she continued. "Are you on your way to Iniston?"

Kova couldn't help but drink in her loveliness as she spoke. The way her tall, slender body moved when she turned to look at him, her barely concealed sensuousness overlaid with a vitality such as only the young can exhibit so effortlessly, all of these things threatened to divert his thoughts and draw them away from her words. It was her face, however, that was most captivating. The sparkle in her eyes as she spoke, the tone of her voice, the gentle flick of her head as she tossed her hair back over her shoulders, she reminded him so much of someone . . . someone who had been very dear to him . . . but no, as quickly as that memory arose, he pushed it away. That wouldn't do at all.

"Ummm . . . yes. I am. This . . . this is a lovely place. Have you been here long?"

"Several years now. I live here with my father. He was a guildsman in Kadrine for many years, but he had to give that away when his eyesight began to suffer. Fortunately, he had saved a bit over the years and so he bought this place and we moved here."

"That's wonderful . . . I mean, it's wonderful that he had the foresight to put something away so he could do that."

"Yes. We have been very lucky. Only . . . I'm a bit worried about him." As she said that, she turned and looked back towards the hills which lay a dozen or more leagues away, beyond the cottage. The broad smile she had at first given Kova had now been displaced by a frown and a clear look of concern. "He's overdue."

"What do you mean, 'overdue'?"

She seemed to hesitate for a moment or so. Then, when she finally responded, it was as if all of the concerns she had been bottling up within her were suddenly given release.

"He left here three days ago now, on a hunting trip, and he hasn't returned. It's not like him. He's never away for more than one night. I'm . . . I'm actually quite worried now. I've been trying to keep busy with gardening and other chores, but it isn't helping. I'm worried that something might have happened to him. He might have fallen and broken a limb, or something like that, and not be able to get back. He might even be lying somewhere injured. I . . . I just don't know whether to go looking for him or to stay here in case he comes back and needs my help. I really don't know what to do."

The plaintive look she gave Kova at that point would have broken the hardest heart. "What about your neighbours?" he asked. "Have you asked them to help you?"

"We're very isolated here. There aren't any other dwellings between us and Iniston. There's no-one I can turn to."

"Oh. That makes it difficult. I can see that. Look, you mustn't worry. I'm sure everything will be alright. Perhaps I could help if you like? Not right at this moment. I *have* to go to Iniston first. I've got some urgent business there that unfortunately just cannot wait. But I could come straight back tomorrow if you want. If your father still isn't back by then, I'll help you go and look for him. Do you have any idea where he went?"

"Oh, thank you, thank you, thank you," Lorelei gushed in obvious relief. "That is so kind. Yes, I know the general direction he headed in. Thank you so much."

"That's okay. My name is Kova. I'll be back as soon as I can in the morning."

"Thank you, Kova. That is so kind. My name is Lorelei. Thank you so very much."

"Don't worry, Lorelei. I'm sure everything will be okay. He probably just sprained his ankle or something simple like that. I'll be back tomorrow." With that, Kova gave her hand a reassuring squeeze, then turned and resumed his journey. When, after he had gone twenty or so paces up the road, he turned to look back again, Lorelei was still standing at the gate, watching him. She gave him a wave and then turned and walked back towards the cottage. Kova resumed his own journey, picking up the pace as he did so. He had a lot to do.

The next day, true to his word, Kova returned. Lorelei was very excited to see him and gave him an unexpected hug, much to his embarrassment. She told him that she'd spent the whole night fluctuating between relief that she'd found someone to help her and concern that he never had any intention of coming back but just didn't want to say so.

Her father still hadn't returned. As it was late morning by the time Kova reached the cottage, they decided to set out straight away. Lorelei was already suitably dressed for a long hike. Apart from a sturdy pair of boots, she had put on a pair of long trousers, a long-sleeved shirt and an oilskin jacket that looked like it would be proof against any bad weather. A wide-brimmed hat and a small backpack completed her outfit. Her long, black hair was tied back in a ponytail. Despite the practical nature of her attire, she looked quite fetching to Kova. She told him that she had water, bandages, and other medical supplies, a rolled-up blanket and sufficient food for an overnight stay in her backpack. As he had also come similarly equipped, with the addition of a sword which was sheathed at his waist, they set out without any further delay.

At first, they followed a trail that led from the back of the property. It took them through a rolling meadow covered in a carpet of wildflowers towards a wooded area a few leagues away. It was the track which Lorelei said her father had taken when he had set out several days earlier. From where they were, Kova could see that the woods continued until they met a small line of hills. The latter were at least a dozen or so leagues distant. He guessed it would be nightfall by the time they got there if they had to go that far.

Both the weather and the trail were kind to them, however, and they made good time at first, reaching the wooded area quite quickly. They slowed a little then. The path twisted and turned as it threaded its way through the trees and Lorelei stopped every now and then to call out, in the hope that if her father was nearby, he might hear her and respond.

She said he had told her once his usual practice was to follow a small stream which could be found only a short distance into the forest. As it flowed down from the distant hills, it widened in several places to form small waterholes before spilling over and continuing its downward flow towards the valley beyond. These waterholes were ideal places to find game, particularly late in the day or in the early morning. Apparently, he would gradually climb up towards the hills, following the stream from one waterhole to the next, until he found the right spot.

Tracks from the many beasts which came down to such places each day would tell him when he had found the best place. Then it would usually be a simple matter of building a hide from fallen branches and the like and waiting until some game appeared. A deer would usually be his preferred target. Though it would be a hard slog carrying the meat back home in his backpack, just one beast would be enough to fill their larder. And so Kova and Lorelei took the same route.

It wasn't long before they had some success. Though he wasn't as experienced a woodsman as her father appeared to be, Kova had done a fair bit of hunting himself, and he knew how to read tracks. When they began to find recent bootprints along a rough track that paralleled the course of the stream, he told her they seemed to be on the right path. Lorelei's relief was palpable.

"Finding some tracks is one thing," Kova cautioned her. "Hopefully this is a good sign, but let's not get too far ahead of ourselves just yet."

"Yes. I know you're right," she responded. "It's just such a relief to be finally doing something after sitting at home worrying day after day."

They pressed on then, alert for any further tracks or signs

her father had been that way. Every now and then, Lorelei would stop and call out, but to no avail. They continued in this fashion for some time and the sun was beginning to approach the horizon when the path they were following began to climb more steeply. They had reached the lower slopes of the hills Kova had seen from a distance earlier in the day.

Just as their hopes of continuing the search that day had begun to fade with the now rapidly failing light, Kova found bootprints again. This time they seemed to veer away from the stream. Looking up in the direction they were headed, he could make out a small opening in the side of the hill above them. From where they stood it was clear it was a small cave, or at least an alcove in which someone could take shelter should the need arise.

Lorelei was convinced they had found the spot where her father must be and made to rush forward when Kova grabbed a hold of her arm to restrain her.

"Let's not rush on up there just yet," he cautioned, seeing the frown of annoyance beginning to form on her face. "A spot like that could easily be the lair of a bear or some other wild beast. Your father might be there, but let's be careful now. If he has got into some difficulty, we won't be much good to him if we do exactly the same."

"Alright," replied Lorelei, drawing a deep breath. She took a long swig from the water flask she'd just retrieved from her pack and then passed it to Kova. "I'm sorry. It's just such a relief. I'm sure he must be in there. I'm glad you're with me, though. I would have gone rushing in if you hadn't been here. Thank you. Even though I keep trying to ignore the thought, I do know it's still possible something bad has happened to him."

"That's alright," Kova responded as she reached out and hugged him to her again. "Any honourable person would have done the same as me.

"I want you to wait for me a bit further down, over near those rocks," he then suggested, drawing his sword as she wiped away the remnants of a tear that had rolled down across her cheek. "I'm going to do a bit of a reconnoitre. Don't worry. I'll be very careful. If something unexpected happens and I come out yelling at you to run, I want you to turn and run back down the hill as fast as you can go. Don't stop until I tell you to and don't worry about me, because if that happens, I'll be right behind you."

Lorelei nodded, glancing towards the cave entrance as she did so as if she now expected some wild creature to come rushing out at them at any moment. As she turned to go back down the trail a half a dozen paces or so, to the spot Kova had indicated, he started to make his own way cautiously up towards the cave.

The path that led up to its entrance was well-worn but the ground there was firmer than that on the trail they'd followed beside the stream. Kova's eyes were on the cave entrance, however, and not on his footing. This was the most dangerous part of the whole enterprise. At least with Lorelei waiting below he would be able to focus solely on what was before him. He also knew that this area was renowned for bear attacks, or so some in Iniston had claimed. His sword wouldn't be of much use if that happened. He'd brought one down once with a bow, but it had taken four arrows. A mature bear would be a formidable foe at close quarters.

He had little choice now. He would just have to be ready for any and every eventuality. Reaching the edge of the opening, he saw that it went back into the hillside some distance. Though he couldn't tell how far it went, there was no doubt that it was a cave and not just an overhang.

Taking a deep breath and summoning all the courage he could muster, he edged forward. Though the entrance to the cavern faced in a southerly direction, a shaft of remaining sunlight coming in from the western side lit his way for the first few paces. That was quickly replaced by a shaded area which then deepened into an inky blackness. As Kova paused to allow his eyes to adjust to the sudden darkness, he cursed himself. The one thing he had not thought to bring was a faggot of wood or something else to use as a torch.

Though his sight was, for the moment at least, hampered, his other senses weren't. A dank musty smell drifted towards the entrance from deep within the cave. Mingled with the dankness, he sensed the merest hint of something else as well, something unusual, unlike anything he'd ever smelt before. It wasn't strong, just an occasional whiff. In normal circumstances he might have thought it was a small animal of some kind, or the remains of something that had crept in here long ago and died.

His hearing seemed to be more acute as well. Though at first he had only been aware of silence, he could now make out the sound of water slowly dripping somewhere, as if it might be dripping from the roof of the cave into a pool of some kind. It was barely audible, which indicated the cave went back some considerable distance.

As he stood there, taking it all in, he found that his eyes had begun to adjust to the darkness. He began to discern shapes which he hadn't been able to see when he had first entered the dark interior. He still couldn't see far, but he could make out some large boulders piled against one wall, only a dozen or so paces from where he stood, as if part of the roof had collapsed there at some point. The floor of the cave tilted slightly after that and the passageway took a turn to the right, denying him any further view of what lay beyond. The area immediately in front of him was littered with twigs and leaf matter, no doubt blown in from the outside by the wind. And there, amongst the twigs and other detritus, right in the middle of the passageway, lay what appeared to be a scarf or a strip of red cloth of some kind.

Keeping his sword arm raised, and a close eye on the area further in, Kova began to edge forward. Someone was here, or had been at least. The cloth was evidence of that, or so it was meant to appear. And it was sitting on top of the leaf matter, not below it, which meant it hadn't been there long. If Lorelei were with him, he was sure she would identify it as her father's.

As he took a few tentative steps towards the cloth, he heard a sharp crack from somewhere below him, and then the ground suddenly moved. He began to fall, grabbing for the sides as he did so, but unable to stop what was happening. For a fraction of a heartbeat his world turned upside down, then a sudden pain stabbed through his thigh, all the air expelled from his lungs in one great whoosh, and a second searing pain caused him to cry out as his head banged against something very hard. For one brief moment, he realised he'd landed on a rough surface, surrounded by utter darkness, with his left arm up against an earthy wall. He felt his consciousness quickly slipping away. His last memory was of a shower of leaf matter and twigs cascading down on him from somewhere up above ... then ... nothing, mercifully, nothing more.

—◁———▷—

Kova wasn't sure how long he'd been unconscious. The sharp pain in his thigh was still there, and he was still sprawled on his back in what he could now see was a deep hole. His left arm still lay against the earthy wall beside him.

The main difference was the two individuals peering down at him from what now appeared to be a well-lit tunnel above where he lay. One was a young man — clearly not Lorelei's father — with jet black hair combed back and tied at the nape of his neck. His pale skin seemed somehow wrong against his dark hair, as if the latter might have been dyed. The other was an old woman. She looked ancient, so ancient he couldn't even hazard a guess at her age.

"Hello there," said the man quite casually, with an amused look on his face. He watched as Kova felt around with his hands for the sword he knew must lie within easy reach. "It's not there. I fished it out while you were having a little nap. You will find a water flask though. Don't worry, it's not drugged like the one Lorelei shared with you before you came up here."

"Drugged? Lorelei drugged me?" It was starting to make some sense, now. His head was woozy, but that was to be expected given the knock he'd taken as he'd fallen into what must have been a trap. But he was feeling tired — unusually tired. He guessed that whatever Lorelei had put in the water she'd shared with him must be starting to take effect.

"Sorry about that, Kova," said the old crone who was kneeling beside the man. "I guess that'll teach you not to put all your trust in a pretty face." As she spoke, it seemed to Kova that he might be about to pass out again. The woman's face, her hair, everything about her, began to blur. When it came back into focus a moment or two later, it was Lorelei who knelt there looking down at him, with a broad smile on her face. She started to laugh and, as the laugh slowly became a horrible cackle, she began to change back again. The whole process took but a few moments.

"Do you still think I'm pretty?" she asked once the transformation back to an old crone was complete. This time, the wicked laugh she gave sent a shudder right down to the core of his soul.

"You'll fall asleep soon," explained the man, once Lorelei had stopped cackling. "Once you do, we'll get you out of there. When you wake up, you're going to find yourself in a cage. I wouldn't worry about that too much if I were you. You can't escape us now. Just make your peace with whatever god you pray to and it'll all be over soon. You've got a nasty few days ahead of you but then it'll all be over."

"But what's this all about? Why are you doing this to me? Who are you?"

"I guess it won't hurt to tell you that now. As for me, I'm what your kind call a leech, though I prefer 'vampyre'. We live off the blood of others. As long as we can get a regular supply, we cannot die. My companion, Lorelei, is a demon, a soul-eater more specifically. Like me, as long as she can get a regular supply of souls she will live forever. And that's what we both intend to do. We've been doing it for centuries now and we intend to go on doing it."

Lorelei broke in at that point. Her voice had a nastier tone. While the man had seemed to be trying to convince him that any attempt at resistance would be futile, she seemed intent on tormenting him.

"Jael will feed from you over the next two or three days," she explained. "Then, it will be my turn. I can't wait to feed on your soul — so young and so full of vitality! Mmmmm. You're going to be quite delicious. I think you're going to be almost as tasty as my last feed. That young woman whose form I've been assuming was one of the best I've ever had. If you're half as delicious as she was, you'll be well worth the wait."

"We've actually got the perfect partnership," boasted Jael, interrupting Lorelei in an obvious attempt to deflect Kova's thought from the picture she had just painted. "Lorelei chooses a victim and lures them up here, well away from prying eyes. Then I capture and bind them. Once that's done, I take my sustenance, and then she takes what she needs. Perfect for us . . . unfortunate for you. That'll teach you to rush in and offer to help a pretty young maiden without checking what you're getting yourself into. I guess you're going to have plenty of time to reflect on that over the next few days."

"I certainly hope so," responded Kova, trying to sit up despite the drowsiness which was beginning to take a hold of him. To Jael's consternation, he seemed not the least bit concerned at the fate that awaited him. "And thank you for clearing that up," he continued. "That filled in most of the gaps for me. Thank you to you too, Lorelei. As painful as it was, I am glad to have seen Aeryn's pretty face again one last time. That was her name, you know — your last victim. She was my fiancé and I will never forget her.

"I've been trying to find her ever since she failed to return from her trip to Iniston some three months past now. She and her father set out to visit his brother there but, sadly, I found out that he fell ill along the way. After a very brief illness, she and his brother buried him there and then she set out to return home. She never made it back, however, as you well know. I followed her trail as best I could and finally narrowed her disappearance down to a small section of the road between Iniston and Faring.

"I spied on your cottage for a while, as it is the only dwelling that can be seen from the road along that stretch. And then, one day, I saw you leaving the house. At first, I thought you were Aeryn, but something made me hold back. When I followed you and saw you head up here, to this cave, I realised that things were not as they seemed. Once I saw you change from Aeryn back to your real self as you approached the cave, my worst fears were confirmed.

"I watched you both then for a time, and while I did, I laid my plans. I returned to my hometown for a while and sought the advice of a wizard whose manse lies not too far from there. Following his instructions, I hired a team of men the wizard assured me had both the skills and the experience to help me carry out my plan. I purchased certain special items that would be needed and then I put it into action. I started by taking that seemingly innocent walk past your cottage.

"That threw me a bit. Seeing you in Aeryn's form from afar was one thing. Standing beside you and chatting was quite another. But I stuck to my plan and . . . well . . . here we are. My men will by now be waiting in the passageway behind you, within earshot, but just out of view.

"When I give the word, they'll come in and take you both captive. Oh, don't worry, I know you'll put up a fight. But these men have done this sort of thing before. There are enough of them and they are armed appropriately to make sure that there will be no escape for the two of you. That was partly why they waited until the both of you were here inside the cave. There is only one way out, as you know only too well.

"As for you, Jael, I guess you know what a princely sum we'll get for your blood once we've drained it from your corpse. How ironic that will be. I must admit I was also surprised to hear that even a vampire's skin is highly sought after. Excellent curative properties so I'm told. Once again, quite ironic really.

"And you, Lorelei. I mustn't forget you. The wizard has told us what we need to do to bind a demon, and guaranteed us a very tidy reward once we deliver you to him. He is quite vain, I think. He says that he intends to keep you . . . alive you'll be pleased to know . . . in a glass jar on his mantlepiece. He said it would be a snug fit, but it can and will be done. It should make quite a demonstration of his power.

"He had no difficulty in agreeing to my special request, however. He has agreed to stand the jar upside down for at least the first century or so.

"That should give *you* ample time to reflect on your past behaviour, don't you think?"

BARNACLE ISLAND

Meira wondered where it would all end, which was curious given that she hadn't yet been able to remember where it had started. She was alone on the island — if indeed the rocky outcropping she now called home was worthy of such a word — that much was certain. As for how she had got there, however, or why, or when, she still had no idea.

She stifled a cry as yet another barnacle pierced the lacerated soles of her feet, interrupting her thoughts as she picked her way across the rocky foreshore. There was simply no way to avoid them, teetering precariously as she searched in vain for places the voracious creatures hadn't claimed as their own, for footholds which didn't demand a tribute in blood.

Like a horde of insatiable, miniature vampires, they lay in wait for her whenever she dared to venture out from her sanctuary beneath the cliff. Drop by drop, they were slowly collecting their toll, their bloody trail only lasting for a few moments, sucked down into their gaping maws until the next surge of the waves washed away the surplus from their merciless feast.

Finally, she made it back to her sanctum. The shawl she longed to throw around her shoulders was sprawled instead across the rocky surface. She scrunched up as tight as she could as she sat down on it, pulling her feet back under her, away from those gluttonous, blood-sucking encrustations. It was wet through, of course, for the spray from the waves was unrelenting, but so was everything else in this godforsaken, hellhole of a prison.

For a prison it was, or as good as. In a sudden moment of clarity, she remembered — that had been why they had left her there. Somewhere in the Sarrowmine Sea; that much at least she did know, for all the good it did her. For, once there, there was no way to leave. They'd sailed away, cursing her as they went, and left her alone, left her with nothing but the wind, and the sea, and the gulls, and the waves, the incessant swell of the waves. They'd left her there to die.

But why? What had she done to deserve it? What kind of people would do such a thing?

I don't know, she thought to herself for the hundredth time that day.

I don't know.

She awoke with a start. She'd dreamt she'd been sitting down to a meal of crabs and fish. The tantalising aroma of the sauce that was draped across the slightly seared fillets had made her mouth water. The bottle of fine wine beside it promised to be the perfect accompaniment. Then, just as she raised the fork to her mouth, just as the divine smell of the perfectly seared harpfish alerted her taste buds to the imminent arrival of something truly wonderful, someone had snatched it away and she'd awoken.

The equally sudden realisation that it was a dream, that she was back in the nightmare that was her existence on this tiny outcrop of rock, surrounded by nothing but waves, waves, and more waves, sent a chill down her spine. It made her want to cry out into the night, to curse those who'd put her there, and all their descendants, forever, even if it was only the gods who would hear her . . . and the fish, and the crabs, though they didn't count. As long as the gods heard her invocation, that would be enough.

But first, please send someone to bring me food, and water, she thought suddenly.

Curses could wait. It was water Meira needed, for she was thirsty beyond all bearing. How long had it been since they'd left her there, without food, without water, with nothing but the clothes on her back and her shawl? Was it hours? Days? Yes, it had been days. She had seen two sunrises since then, or was it three? Three, that's right. But . . . wasn't one of those a sunset? She was no longer sure. Her mouth was so dry she was finding it difficult to swallow. Just trying brought a sharp stabbing pain to the back of her throat. Her lips were cracking too. She'd tried to keep them moist by rubbing seawater across them from time to time but that had only made it worse.

She'd tried drinking it too — the seawater, that is. Its briny smell permeated every part of her surroundings, but she had to drink something. At first, it had been a glorious relief. Finally, to have water, and so much of it that she need never worry again. She'd always been told that you couldn't drink it but she wondered then why they had lied. Until she threw it all up again. Until she retched until her stomach was empty.

She'd tried again a little while later when her thirst became all-consuming once more. How could she resist? She was, after all, surrounded by it. Perhaps, she thought, her body just needed to accustom itself to the saltiness. But it was no good. She vomited again, and then her head began to ache. It still ached. A constant dull throbbing, as if there was something inside her, pounding on her temples, trying to get out.

Sleep. That was what she needed. She was so weary still, anyway. Perhaps when she woke up she'd remember why they had been so heartless.

I don't know, she thought, as she drifted off.

I don't know.

◆————————◆

It was the sun that woke her. In the mornings it streamed in despite the overhang. She hated the mornings. The sun baked her skin, cracking her lips, burning her forehead. There was no escaping it. Finally, in desperation, Meira pulled her blouse up over her head. The skin around her stomach would burn, but at least, for a while, her head would be protected.

If only there were somewhere else to go in the mornings. But there wasn't. The whole island was only thirty-seven paces long at its widest point. She knew. She'd counted them, many times. And anyway, she couldn't bear to face those pitiless barnacles anymore.

They were everywhere. Perhaps, she thought, that was what she should call the island — Barnacle Island. They owned it, after all. They'd still be there when she was gone.

Who knows? Maybe that was already its name.

Probably not, she thought. *It may not even have a name. I think it would have to be bigger to be given a name. It's my island now, though. So, I can name it. I can call it anything I like. I declare this island 'Barnacle Island'. There. It's done.*

A crab scurried across the rocks just a hand's breadth away from her toes. *If only I could catch one*, she thought. *Then at least I'd have something to eat. I'll die here if I can't get something to eat.*

Of course, she knew, that was what they intended — those who had left her there. They meant for her to die there. They had consigned her to a horrible death, with nothing to drink, and nothing to eat. How cruel. But why would they do that, she wondered. What had she done to them?

Sometimes she thought she might be able to remember. She thought about it often enough. It was one of the best ways to take her thoughts away from her hunger and her thirst. And strangely, the wearier she became, the closer she seemed to get to recovering the memory. It was like a book now. She could see the book in her mind when she tried to remember what had happened.

That was progress. Before the book, there had been nothing . . . nothing but empty space, a void. But that was before . . . before she had found the book that held her memory. It was a step forward. Only a small one, for when she turned the pages, they were all blank. It was a beginning, nonetheless. She felt sure the memory wanted to come back.

She just needed to be patient.

A movement just at the edge of her field of vision interrupted her thoughts again. *I see you little crab. Just you wait. Oh yes, think you're clever, don't you, running out like that while I'm looking the other way? But you're going to make a mistake soon. And then I'll get you. Then I'll eat you.*

Oh, what did I do? Why are the pages all blank?

I don't know.

I don't know.

Meira slept again for a while. It might have been an hour, or it might have been two days. There was no way to tell. What did it matter anyway?

The book, once she'd found it, was where she spent most of her time now. She felt better there. The hunger that gnawed at her stomach, her dry, rasping throat, the blisters on her face and arms, and her legs; she could forget all of those while she poured over the book.

Her body didn't exist when she was in that place, and so she retreated to it more and more. And as she did so, the words slowly began to emerge. The pages started to fill. It was a slow process — a sentence first, then another. Gradually, more began to appear, a whole page, then two.

She devoured the words as soon as they turned up. Food for her mind that somehow assuaged the hunger she felt in her body, for a while, at least.

It was a story. Meira's husband, Keryd, was in it. He was a carter. She knew that without reading it in the book. He worked for the merchants down at the wharves. When the big trading vessels came in, he and the other carters would load up the big sacks, onto their backs usually, but sometimes onto small carts. Then they would carry them up into the town, to the stores and other merchants they were intended for. Once that was done, they would go back down to the wharf and fetch another load.

It was back-breaking work. Inevitably, Keryd would be exhausted when he came home. Meira would have his meal ready for him, and they would sit quietly chatting together while they ate. He was a good man, a good provider. And she played her part too. During the day, while he was carting loads, she would be at the fullers, helping to clean the wool before it went off to the weavers. That was hard work too. But it helped fill the days, and their purse. With the money they earned between them, life was good. Hard, but good.

That's what the first few pages were about. It didn't explain why they'd put her there, but it was a beginning. She wanted to read more. She needed to know why they had brought her to this island then sailed away so cruelly and left her there. Why had they done that?

What did I do? I don't know. Maybe the book will tell me. It must. Because I don't know.

I don't know.

Meira felt a little better when she woke again. Her stomach felt like it was one big empty hole though, which, in a sense, was precisely what it was. It ached constantly and was sensitive to touch, so she tried her best to forget it.

Her thirst was more demanding, however. The ache in her head had worsened, and she had begun to see things which she knew weren't really there — friends from her past, Keryd, her father. She wondered if she was beginning to lose her mind. She had to do something.

She tried to drink from the small pool of water near where she lay. It looked so clear and enticing. Perhaps all the salt has settled to the bottom, she thought, and she could scoop the fresh water off the top. And so she did. She threw up again within a few moments, or tried to at least. There was nothing in her stomach to throw up anymore. The water she'd drank, of course, but nothing else, not even bile.

She rolled over, closed her eyes, and opened the book again. Some more words had appeared. She read on.

Anything to take her mind off her bloated stomach and her throbbing head.

Keryd had started coming home later than usual. Once or twice a week at first. Then more frequently. Three nights in a row on one occasion. He said that several ships had come in at the same time and there was more work than the carters could cope with.

But she hadn't seen any extra ships. She worked during the day, but she could always see the masts above the roofs of the houses and other buildings when she returned to their home at dusk. She hadn't seen any extra masts.

He started to change, as well. Only in the smallest of ways, at first, but a wife knows these things. He became more distant. She began to worry. What was he up to? She decided to follow him.

The page after that was blank. She had to find out the rest. What had he been up to? Why had they put her there? She was still none the wiser.

I don't know, she thought, wondering absently if the fluid in the blisters that were forming all over her arms might help slake her thirst.

I don't know.

It's the water, Meira concluded when she awoke next. The water was helping her to remember. She was sure of it. It was making her sick, she knew that, but whenever she drank some of it, she would drift off into a haze and more of the words would come back.

She cupped her hands in the small rock-pool and drank deeply. It came back up almost as quickly as it went down. She lay back. Her side was hurting but she had no idea why. She had to close her eyes. Everything was moving. For a moment, she thought the island was sinking. She tried to think of the book and nothing else. If the island sank beneath the waves, then at least it would all be over. But it didn't. She felt a calmness come over her. The world settled back onto its foundations again. She opened the book and read on.

She followed Keryd one evening. She went down to the wharf, stood back in the shadows, and waited for him to come out of the warehouse with his load on his back. It was such a load — three huge sacks. More, surely, than one man could carry. His muscles rippled as he bore it. She loved him so. She felt the stirrings of arousal just watching him, almost cast off her doubts and ran out and begged him to come home with her right that instant. But she didn't. She held back. She followed him. She felt terrible doing that, not trusting him. But it was good that she didn't.

After he delivered his load, on his way back, he took a

turn away from the wharf. He stopped at a house in a narrow street, away from the main thoroughfare, and knocked on the door. Someone opened it. She heard a woman's voice, then a laugh, and a slender hand reached out and pulled him inside. She went up to the windows, but she couldn't see in. All of the curtains were closed. But she heard them laughing.

That hurt. She felt that something precious had been taken from her and given to someone else — the laughter and closeness which till then had been such a special part of their relationship was now being shared with another. It left her feeling empty — hollow. An overwhelming sense of loss consumed her. She sobbed all the way back to her home.

Meira stopped reading then. She didn't want to think about it anymore. The next page was blank anyway.

Some sleep, she thought. Then, when she woke up, she would catch a few of those crabs and cook them, sauté them with butter and garlic. She'd meant to do that yesterday, but it must have slipped her mind

But . . . but if Keryd betrayed his vows, then he should be here, not her.

Why isn't he here instead of me?

I don't know.

She was awake but didn't want to open her eyes. It was still dark. She could tell that, even with her eyelids closed. She opened the book. She didn't want to, but she had to know. She had to read on. It had become a compulsion.

When Keryd returned that night, she said nothing about having followed him. Perhaps it hadn't been what it appeared to be. She had to be sure. So, she followed him again two nights later. He went to that woman's house again. This time she waited until he came out. When he finally did, he stood there tucking his shirt into his trousers as he was saying his goodbyes.

Unfortunately, from where she was standing there was no clear view of the face of the woman who stood in the doorway chatting to him. There was no mistaking the warmth of their embrace, however, as he leaned back in and hugged her, then turned to walk away. The woman's parting words cut right through to her heart. 'Goodnight, my love,' she called out before she closed the door. And there was no mistaking her tone. It was that of a satisfied woman, of a sweetheart farewelling her lover.

Meira opened her eyes then, needing to wrench her thoughts away from the book. It was too upsetting. She wanted to cry but couldn't. There wasn't enough fluid left within her body for tears to form.

She decided it would be best to end it all. She would drag herself down to the water and throw herself in. That would be it. She was too weak to have any chance of saving herself once she was in the water, even if she wanted to. But she barely had the strength to get down to the water's edge. She was tired. So very tired. Perhaps a few moments of rest first. Some more sleep. Just a little nap.

It's not right, she thought, as her consciousness slipped away. *Why did they put me here? Why not him? Why not her? I don't know.*

I don't know.

✦————✦

It was morning. At least she thought so. In the dim light everything seemed to blur. She reached up with her hands and felt her eyes. They were open, but everything was still foggy. Where was she?

On the island, she suddenly remembered. They put me on Barnacle Island. She'd heard someone call it that, she was sure.

Her vision began to fade again. Her surroundings began to disappear. She found herself in a void. There was nothing there except for a wooden table . . . and a book. It was her book. It had been left open. She leaned over and began to read it again.

After that night, she waited, hoping Keryd would have his fling and then come back to her. Men were like that. Cruel. Selfish. That was the way of the world. Things would never be the same between them again, but at least she would have him back.

Perhaps the woman had seduced him, given him one of those potions they say the witches will sell you. She might have met him at a tavern and slipped something into his drink to make him desire her. He was a good man. They meant everything to each other. He wouldn't do something like that without having been tricked into it.

She began to hate the woman. It was her fault. She thought of all the terrible things she wished might befall her. She worked herself up into a frenzy. She decided to confront her. She made excuses to leave her work early one afternoon. The fuller was angry, but she wouldn't listen. She went straight to the woman's house and knocked on the door. The woman opened the door. She was young . . . and pretty, a girl really, barely a woman at all. She hadn't expected that. She could only have been half her own age.

'What are you talking about?' the girl demanded when confronted with what she had done. Her brazen denial was shocking. That, and the reckless way she laughed at the accusation. Meira couldn't bear it. She could feel the blood pumping madly against her temple as if it wanted to burst right out of her. As the girl turned to go back inside, Meira pulled a knife from her pocket and stabbed her in the back of her neck. She stabbed her again in her back, and again, and again, and again, and again. She kept stabbing her as she fell, then stood there, her chest heaving, looking down at the body at her feet and the blood that was spattered across her dress, on the floor, on the wall. There was blood everywhere.

Dimly at first, she became aware that someone was screaming. It was the high-pitched scream of a child. A young girl stood at the foot of a staircase. She could only have been four or five years old. The screaming wouldn't stop. Meira took two steps, then grabbed hold of the girl's hair, pulled back her head and slashed the knife across her throat. The scream became a gurgle, then stopped as the girl's body slumped to the floor as well.

She looked around at what she had done, then calmly turned and left the house. The knife in her hand dripped a trail of blood as she wandered down the street.

They told her later that the girl she had killed wasn't the one her husband had been meeting. That woman had left the day before. She had found out that Keryd was married. He had told her he was a widower. The woman couldn't bear the thought of having betrayed a married woman. She quickly packed and left town. She asked the young girl who lived in a lodging-house up the street if she would keep a watch on her home while she was away. She told her that she could bring her daughter with her.

Meira had killed the wrong woman . . . and her daughter. The magistrate said there was no precedent for how to punish such a crime. He said they should leave her fate to the gods, that hers was too wicked a crime for mere mortals to judge. They took her out to the island and left her there . . . to die.

Sailors knew the island well, they said. Many a crew had gone to a watery grave when the howling gales of a winter storm had cast their vessel upon its shoreline. Karnath's Doorstep they called it, the gateway to the lord of the underworld's domain. It was a fitting place for someone such as her. As they sailed away, one of them cried out to her, 'Let Karnath take you now. There is no place for you amongst your fellows any longer.'

Meira could feel his contempt again now, stabbing into her very soul as the scene replayed in her thoughts. She turned her head towards the rocks beneath her — dry retching.

I didn't know.

She summoned up the last remnants of her energy and began to drag herself towards the water.

I didn't know.

A trail of blood marked her route as she passed as the barnacles cut her hands and feet to shreds.

I didn't know.

Finally, she reached the water and slipped in.

I didn't know.

A wave washed over her, filling her open mouth with its salty cargo as she slipped beneath its surface.

I didn't know.

I didn't know.

I didn't know.

THE SEVEN TOWERS OF
TRINKOLAI

I t was in the year of the 373rd Summer of the New Age
that construction first began on the towers that would,
in time, earn Trinkolai the reputation of having one of
the most breathtaking skylines in all of Ilythia. Situated at the
mouth of the River Morn, and overlooking a picturesque
harbour, the preeminence it already held as principal city of
Beirinya, one of the three great powers of the time, would
be nothing compared to the fame it would earn as the home
of the Seven Towers.

The latter quickly became the most notable architectural
wonders of the New Age and drew vast multitudes of

incredulous visitors to the city from the furthermost corners of the world. In the years following their completion, the market in the sale of soothing ointments for tourists suffering muscle cramp from constantly craning their necks upward to gaze at the towering edifices was alone enough to guarantee the financial security of many a previously struggling Trinkolite entrepreneur. The myriad other benefits from what came to be an ongoing influx of visitors, each intent on seeing for themselves those renowned structures, has made Trinkolai what it remains today — the richest and most cosmopolitan metropolis in all of Ilythia.

What could not have been foreseen was that the year construction commenced would also mark the beginning of the downfall of House Tamear, and lead to an eventual calamity which, though you will never find any written history of the event, is even to this day as unsurpassed as is the wonder of the towers.

Ravaryn II, King of Beirinya, first formed a desire to construct a magnificent tower while on a visit to Trest, in neighbouring Helidos. The occasion was the holding of the Pelanthion Games which, in every third year, precede the annual Fair of the Turning. The Fair, itself one of the major events of its kind in Ilythia, is held over a two-week period halfway between the summer and winter solstices.

In the year of the 372nd Summer of the New Age, the richest man in all of Ilythia, one Nikos Darven, then head of the most successful of the great Helidorian commercial houses, invited the cream of Ilythian society to attend the wedding of his only daughter, Nesrin.

Darven was Beirinya's largest financial benefactor. Without his support during its recently concluded war with Kaj, Beirinya would undoubtedly have come out on the wrong end of that titanic struggle and ended up nothing more than a Kaji vassal state. Any wonder then that Ravaryn thought it beholding upon him to accept the entrepreneur's invitation.

Besides, he had never previously attended either the Fair or the Games. Beirinya also had high hopes that one of its own citizens, the great Haldron, might carry off the prized brooch, the famed Silver Wheel. If so, that would be the icing on the cake for a trip which promised to be most entertaining while at the same time fulfilling a host of diplomatic and political obligations.

It was while in Trest, on a tour of the local sites with several other grandees, that Ravaryn first beheld the latest addition to the Helidorian capital's Halls of Devotion. The Halls were widely admired, as much for the serene sanctity of their richly appointed interiors as for their egalitarian purpose. They never closed. No matter what the time of day, they provided a refuge for any adherent of the four principal Ilythian gods, the Ilaroi, regardless of his or her social standing.

All were alike once they crossed the threshold, from the lowest, penniless, beggar to those of the very highest rank, including the five Councillors who ruled Helidos. Even a king, such as Ravaryn, might find a street urchin kneeling beside him as he knelt before one of the four altars . . . and be expected to accept that as their right. Outside, on the streets, of course, was an entirely different matter.

As if the building wasn't already glorious enough for their liking, the Council of Five had recently commissioned the addition of a grand tower which had been constructed in a way that enabled devotees from any of the four separate halls to ascend, by means of intricately entwined stairways, some forty spans to its apex. Once there, worshippers found that the small chamber at the top provided no view of the surrounding city. Small grates allowed for the influx and egress of air, but nothing more. A simple wooden bench ringed its walls. The chamber was designed to provide a sanctuary for reflection for the faithful, not for sightseers.

What caught Ravaryn's attention most, however, wasn't the increased opportunity for devotion afforded by the new tower. It was its height. As far as anyone knew, this was the tallest structure in the whole of Ilythia.

From the moment the King first saw it, a desire formed within him to append something even grander, that is, *higher*, to Trinkolai's royal palace. After all, flushed with their success in the recent Kaj-Beirinyan War, what better statement of his country's renewed prominence could there be?

And so it was that Ravaryn summoned Petronus, Master

of the Guild of Builders, to his audience chamber on the very day he returned to Beirinya. Haldron's lack of success at the games had only strengthened the King's determination to put Beirinyan supremacy beyond doubt.

"My liege," offered Petronus, striving not to sound too obsequious. The Master Builder had donned his best formal attire and hastily scampered across the city in great trepidation upon receiving notice that his attendance was required at the palace. It was late and he had been abed when the royal messenger had arrived at his villa. He dreaded to think what could be wrong. His most recent project, the installation of new city gates, had not only been completed ahead of schedule; they had, if anything, exceeded all expectations. The King himself had sung their praises. What could have happened since then to cause the King to issue a summons at such a late hour?

"How may I be of assistance, my lord," he queried in the most respectful voice he could muster, as he bowed so low it took all of his will to stop from toppling forward.

"I want a tower," demanded the King.

"A tower, my lord? I thought you said the walls already have sufficient towers and that only the gates needed strengthening? Or do you mean at the harbour entrance? That would certainly be a boon to defence from the sea."

"No. No. Nothing like that. Did I say anything about the walls, or the harbour? Damn it, man! I want a tower that rises above the royal palace. And it must be no less than fifty spans high, from the ground to its top — whatever you call that — its pinnacle. Is that the right term? Can you do it?"

Petronus took a deep breath, feeling the tension easing out of him. He wasn't about to lose his head. The King had simply formed another of his whims. Unfortunately, this one now seemed to be on the verge of becoming an order, despite its thin disguise as a request. He would still need to tread carefully. "Certainly, my lord. Fifty spans is a very great height, though. I'm not sure that is possible. I don't think anyone has ever built anything that high."

"They haven't. That's the point man. Fifty spans. You have four days to come back to me with plans. You may go."

Yes, my lord." The Master slowly backed out of the chamber, maintaining his bowed stance as he did so and hoping he wouldn't bump into one of the guards or a pillar or something before he found the door. *A tower*, he was thinking, *fifty spans high! Why do the gods torment me so?*

And thus began the project to build the first of Trinkolai's great towers.

As requested, the Master Builder returned with sketches of the proposed new tower within the four days allotted. He was no fool. He knew the best way to keep one's head was to give a ruler of Ravaryn II's temperament what he wanted, especially when his 'requests' were presented as forcefully as this one had been. He also knew, however, that the King was not a builder. The 'plans' he presented to Ravaryn were simply broad sketches of what the finished tower might look like. While preparations were being made, and a suitable team was being assembled, Petronus' real task would now begin. He had to work out how to build a tower fifty spans high — something that had never been done before.

The rest is history, as they say. Petronus did find a way to build Ravaryn's tower. It took all of his ingenuity, and a few false starts, but, with the resources of the monarchy behind him, he got there in the end. And in typical manner, he showed why it was that he, of all the builders in Beirinya, was chosen to hold the Royal Warrant. For, once again, he exceeded Ravaryn's requirements. Not only did he build a tower at least fifty spans high — fifty-three spans actually, not that anyone was counting, except Ravaryn of course — but the way the new structure augmented the existing palace complex was so cunningly done it enhanced the latter's already considerable beauty as well. Ravaryn got more than the highest tower in the land. He got an extended palace complex which was the envy of all as well.

And so it was that Ravarayn II beamed with pride as he stood before his courtiers on the day of the tower's consecration, little more than a year after he had first formed the desire to see it done. His wife, the Queen, stood proudly beside him, though half a step back, as is natural, as did his two young sons, Ravaryn— who it was hoped would one day be Ravaryn III — and Jaspyr.

"Remember this day," the King advised them earnestly, turning to look down at his young progeny as he spoke.

"Beirinya is the greatest nation Ilythia has ever seen. Our family — House Tamear — rules it. And *this* is how we do it.

"My goal," he went on, warming to his homily, "right from the day of my coronation, was to be an even greater ruler than my father had been. That is what a great ruler does. He strives to be the greatest of all rulers, to surpass everyone who has come before him. Of course, I realise that, with my achievements, I have made that impossible for the two of you, but never mind, strive to do great things, nonetheless.

"Mark my words," he continued. "This tower will stand for many centuries as a monument to my achievements. Already they are calling me 'Ravaryn the Builder'. I like that. Greatness doesn't come to you just because you sit on a gilded throne, you know. You have to go out and earn it. You have to do great things. Make your mark on the pages of history. Remember that if you remember nothing else."

And they did — remember his words, that is.

In due course, Ravaryn III ascended the throne as his father's successor. He was only twenty-four years old. A bare sixteen years had passed since the day he had stood behind his father, listening to those words, and seeing his father's claims reflected in the obvious pride of the surrounding courtiers.

As children, he and his brother had both adopted the competitive spirit the King had ever encouraged with all the enthusiasm one might have expected from two overindulged young princes growing up in a fawning royal court. And the old saying — look to the deeds of the child, for they are the seeds of the man — held true as they emerged into adulthood. But in one way, at least, which the father had not expected.

Only a week had passed since the coronation when Petronus found himself unexpectedly summoned before the new king. The years had not been kind to the Master Builder. Though he had come to rely on his team of young able-bodied men even more than ever, the days when he had clambered up and down the frames himself and pitched in to help hoist the big stones or to relay heavy buckets from the ground up to the highest level had all taken their toll. He now walked with a marked stoop and the aid of a cane. Though the body was less willing than days gone by, however, he had lost none of his acumen, or his caution, when dealing with the royal personage.

"All praise to you my lord," smoothed the Master Builder, bowing as low as his ageing body would permit. "How may I be of assistance?"

"I want a tower," demanded the new king with a hint of determination in his voice that instantly reminded the builder of his late predecessor.

"Yes, my lord. Where should I build this tower, my lord?"

"Right beside the existing palace. Demolish Viscount Malerik's house and build it there. His estate is to be incorporated into the royal demesne. He won't be needing it anymore. I've just appointed him the new ambassador to the Algarian court."

"Yes, my lord," responded Petronus, wondering what would become of the rest of Malerik's family. Where would they live if his estate was incorporated into the palace complex?

"And one other thing."

"Yes, my lord."

"Make it at least sixty spans high. When I stand at the top, I expect to be looking down on my father's tower, and I want everyone to see that. Is that clear?" From the time he was a young boy, right through to his coming of age, Raveryn had never forgotten his father's assertion that his successors would never be able to match his achievements.

"Yes, my lord."

And with that, a second great project swung into action.

Petronus, of course, had no doubts about his ability to successfully complete this new commission. He stood at the very top of his profession. Though the first tower was still a stupendous achievement, and was acknowledged as such far and wide, he had thought often over the years about how it had been done, and of the ways he could have gone even higher still if he had his time over again. It wouldn't be easy, but alone of all the builders in Ilythia, he knew that he could do it.

And he did. The second tower was duly completed in 391. It measured sixty-one spans, from the ground to its highest point. The endeavour was not without its consequences, however. No more than one might expect from such a grand undertaking, but consequences, nonetheless.

On the positive side, Ravarayn III 's reputation, along with Petronus' and Trinkolai's, was greatly enhanced, as had been intended. To be the home of the most famous structure in the land, an outstanding architectural feature in its own right, putting aside its vertical attributes, was one thing. To then see another even higher and more amazing structure constructed almost beside the first made Trinkolai, once again, the talk of Ilythia.

On the negative side, the fallout included the loss of one Viscount, one Holder of the Keys to the Royal Coffers and seven young apprentice masons. Though their families, and Petronus, greatly grieved the latter, the royal court paid no heed to their passing at all. The king laughed dismissively at the Master Builder's request for a pension for the four widows created by the accident which had led to the apprentices' demise. In disgust, Petronus paid for the funerals and funded the pensions out of his own pocket.

As for Viscount Malerik, the paltry compensation he received in return for the crown's resumption of his Trinkolite property, coming at a time when he had already racked up a rather unfortunate number of debts, pushed his House to the verge of ruin. Unfortunately, the injudicious financial transactions he then entered into in a vain attempt to relieve the situation were too hastily contracted. When one of his enemies brought them to the attention of the royal personage, his fate was sealed. Called home from Algeria for urgent talks after only two seasons, the last thing he heard was the collective gasp from the excited crowd of onlookers as the executioner swung his mighty axe high up into the air above his outstretched neck.

The Holder of the Keys to the Royal Coffers was grateful, therefore, to simply lose his job. His crime was to have been overheard talking to a fellow courtier.

"If these kings build too many more of these ridiculous towers they'll empty the royal coffers," he had exclaimed to the wrong person. "I don't want to spend my final years as Holder of the Keys trying to find ways to fill them up again, like I had to after that ill-conceived war with Kaj."

And so, he didn't — spend his final years that way, that is. He accepted the King's 'suggestion' that he make way for a younger man and retired to his estate in Talir, grateful not only to have kept his head attached to his body but to have saved his family from ruin and dishonour.

He was not the only one, however, whose career came to an earlier than expected end. Ravaryn III's reign also came to an abrupt halt when he was only forty-nine, just as he'd begun to talk of finding a pretext for another war with Kaj. His father had won a great victory against that traditional Beirinyan enemy, and he was determined to outdo that as well. His goal was to extend Beirinya's borders beyond the Dark River, a truly ambitious aim.

A tower was one thing, but this was a step too far. Shortly after first voicing his thoughts on this new endeavour, he and his brother, the then Prince, Jaspyr, stayed up late one night with a few bottles of fine Kardonian White. In the early hours of the next day, when the only servant who had been in attendance returned from a quest for another flagon or two, he found Jaspyr leaning over the prostrate body of the King. Ravaryn had, apparently, slipped while attempting to get up from the table they had both been seated at and had knocked the back of his head against the edge of the table as he had fallen. It had been a fatal blow.

The servant in question, who had noticed a blood-stained candlestick holder sitting curiously out of place on a small table below a nearby window, disappeared from the palace a few days later and was never heard of again. Though no one, not even his own family, knew it, Jaspyr had provided him with a tidy sum as the stake for a new life in the recently tamed frontier on Tenamos — in the Southern Marches.

Upon his death, as Ravaryn III and his wife, Alyse, had two daughters, the Princesses Julia and Nilsa, but no male heirs, his brother, Jaspyr I, ascended to the throne of Beirinya. He was forty-six years old, and it was the Year of the 414th Summer of the New Age.

Unlike Ravaryn, Jaspyr proved to be a prudent king. He knew from the recently appointed Holder of the Keys to the Royal Coffers that the country's finances were in a parlous state. In order to rectify the situation, he tightened the royal belt, imposed a moderate increase on customs duties for goods entering Beirinya from abroad, and generally gave the new Holder of the Keys a free hand in improving the financial situation, all the while ensuring as much of the burden as possible fell on external traders, and not on his own subjects.

By the time he turned sixty, in 428, the kingdom was back in the black. His had been an uneventful reign, but one that the country had sorely needed.

To mark the occasion of his sexagesimal birthday, he loosened the purse strings slightly and threw a grand party. It was an important day in his life, and not just because he had survived into what would be a seventh decade. It was the day he first really noticed his young niece — Nilsa.

His much-loved wife of many years had lived to be his queen, but had passed away when he was but fifty, only four years after he had been crowned. Though theirs had been a childless marriage, that hadn't mattered while his brother was king. Regardless of that one regret, their love had been genuine and deep, a rare thing indeed amongst the Beirinyan nobility. And so, when Queen Merryn had died, Jaspyr had determined to live out his remaining days as a bachelor. Ten years, and Nilsa, changed all of that.

A whirlwind courtship followed, for Nilsa returned his attentions. She was a widow herself, and childless too, but she liked the thought of being Jaspyr's queen, something she had never dreamt would be possible. They married within a few months of his birthday and were very happy together, despite some twenty years or so difference in their ages.

They had only been married for three years, and Jaspyr's health had begun to show the first signs that his seventh decade may very well be his last, when Nilsa began to talk to him about his legacy. He had no heir, and his reign had been largely uneventful. While the kingdom's finances had recovered and were now, once more, on a solid footing, his reign, she said, would be seen by historians as decidedly unremarkable.

"Why don't you commission a third tower?" she suggested one day. "The country can afford it. Just two, though each grand in their own way, looks rather odd. Incomplete in some way. But three — that has a roundness to it that seems just right to me."

She got quite excited then. "We could dedicate it to Sarkan. Of all of the Ilaroi, he seems to attract the least number of worshippers. That would make it really stand out. And, of course, it would have to be taller than the other two. No doubt that can be done." Nilsa knew nothing about building but thought it should be a simple matter to repeat what had already been done, and then just add a few additional spans. That didn't sound too difficult to her.

As time went on, Nilsa, having conceived the notion, never let it go. At first, Jaspyr discounted it out of hand. But as the years passed, and his health continued to deteriorate, he found himself thinking about his legacy more and more. Finally, he succumbed to his wife's urging.

Petronus' son, Arthron, had by then succeeded the builder of the first two towers and taken on the mantle of Master Builder. In 434, he accepted a commission from Jaspyr I to construct a third tower to adorn the royal palace in Trinkolai.

Arthron proved to be the equal, if not a greater builder than his father, completing the new tower in 436. It stood seventy-two spans tall. Jaspyr lived to see its completion, but only just. He passed away only two months after its consecration. Nilsa lived on until she joined him in the royal mausoleum in 453. By then, she was sixty-three years old.

More than seventy years passed before the Kings of Beirinya found themselves, yet again, in the grip of 'tower-fever', as the cannier Trinkolites came to call it. Two further generations had sat on the throne during that time.

First came Marlan, Nilsa's nephew, who was himself

descended from Ravaryn II's father, Petyr IV. He was only nineteen in 436 when he took the crown following the death of Jaspyr. After a long reign, his son, Jaspyr II, succeeded him in 489. When he passed away in 504, he in turn was succeeded by his second son, Petyr V. It was then that the madness began in earnest once again.

Petyr had married Asena, the headstrong daughter of a powerful Beirinyan duke, in 497, while his father was still king. Theirs was not a union born of true love, however. Asena's seduction of and subsequent marriage to the then prince was just the first step along a road she had mapped out while still in her teens; its ultimate goal the construction of a fourth tower which would not only dwarf all of the others, but which would bear her name. Her dream was for it to be known throughout Ilythia as the Asenan Tower. With that in mind, having secured his hand in marriage, Asena began to stoke the flames of desire for another tower within her husband's heart.

It didn't take long for her plans to show signs of bearing fruit. Petyr was never going to be a strong leader, as she well knew when she first set her sights upon him as a teenager. He was easily led. In the hands of a skilled manipulator the likes of Asena, with no qualms about adding all of her not inconsiderable feminine charms to the mix whenever she deemed it necessary, he never stood a chance. He didn't even know he had been manipulated. Within year or so, he was convinced that it was, in fact, his idea. He even took pride in having overcome his wife's resistance to his suggestion that the tower be named after her.

While on the face of it, she was in reluctant agreement with what he truly believed was *his* plan, Asena covertly maintained the pressure over the years, sustaining his determination whenever it looked like flagging to enact his plan as soon as he gained the throne.

And so, on midsummer's eve in 504, a bare three weeks after he had ascended the throne as King Peter V of Beirinya, he summoned the Master Builder and commissioned the construction of a fourth tower.

Within days Trinkolai was abuzz with excitement. The only Beirinyans who had been alive when the last tower had been completed had been children at the time. The realisation that the wondrous three towers, conceived and built by their ancestors, would soon be four, thrilled the nation. People broke into applause whenever the king appeared in public.

"The four towers of Trinkolai," some called out as he passed; and the call would then be taken up by others.

"Long live Petyr," cried others. "Petyr the Great."

"Mishra's tower," some shouted. "Build Mishra's Tower."

For that was his plan — to let everyone believe it was his intention to dedicate the tower to Mishra and then, when it was completed, declare a change of heart, having come to the realisation that, regardless of the precedent which had been established by his ancestors, such a dedication would clearly be an unworthy presumption. No structure built by mere mortals could be worthy of a god. He would change the dedication then and name the tower after his Queen instead. Asena's Tower it would be from then and forever more.

"Men!" complained Queen Asena to her lady-in-waiting as she was dressing for a ball to be held one evening. Only an hour earlier, the guards had been forced to clear a path for their carriage through cheering crowds on their return to the palace from their country residence. "They are so competitive. That's all this tower is about. Petyr just wants to show he can do things bigger and better than anyone else. It's always about having a faster horse, a faster chariot, a bigger royal barge, to piss further, to have a bigger willy than anyone else. They're like children really. I'll just have to let him have his way, I suppose

"Not that one," she snapped harshly, suddenly interrupting the chain of her idle patter as her assistant brought out her emerald necklace. "I'll wear the gold chain tonight. The rubies should set off my new hair colouring. I'll be the envy of every woman there. Don't you think? This auburn rinse is all the rage in Trest. It'll set a new trend for our court tonight. I'm sure of it. They'll all be rushing off to get one once they've seen me tonight."

And so, once again, in the year of the 506th Summer of the New Age, the Beirinyan court gathered to celebrate the consecration of yet another tower rising above the royal palace in Trinkolai. Though there were a few murmurs, and the applause was, for just a few moments, uncertain, in the end, they cheered long and loud at the naming of the grand new structure. Asena's Tower. Ninety-two spans high. A new record, for a new tower, to herald a new ruler, and a new century.

The ensuing party lasted far into the night. Indeed, it was still going way into the wee hours of the next day. For in two things at least, Beirinyans excelled all others. They knew how to party. And they knew how to build towers.

◆———◆

Unfortunately, it transpired that the king's body was as weak as Asena had so astutely judged his character to be. After a reign which lasted a mere fifteen years, Petyr V succumbed to pneumonia and died aged forty-five, leaving behind his wife and their young son, Hagan, who inherited his crown.

Apart from his one outstanding achievement — construction of the fourth tower — Petyr's rule had been an ineffective one on several fronts. The kingdom's financial situation had taken a body blow during his tenure with a constant stream of architectural follies put forward by his scheming wife slowly draining the coffers with little to show for the investment. The most notable of these, without any shadow of a doubt, was the solid gold life-sized statue of the queen which looked down from its gilded plinth upon all who entered the richly adorned hall which sat at the base of Asena's Tower.

Beirinya's relationship with its neighbour, Verinor, had also deteriorated rapidly over the course of his reign. The speed of that decline was only matched by the depth of Asena's disdain for her Verinorian counterpart. Taniya, consort to the King of Verinor, was widely admired for both her great beauty and her gentle nature. She was the epitome of what most Ilythians saw as the ideal queen. Asena hated her.

From the moment she first set eyes upon the Queen during a state visit to Beirinya by the Verinorian monarch shortly after the fourth tower had been completed, she determined to sow the seeds of distrust between their two kingdoms. She had looked on, seething with anger, as the Beirinyan nobles, her own husband included, had flocked admiringly around the visiting King's beautiful young consort. She determined to never let that happen again. And it didn't.

Now, with a new monarch, her son, Hagan I, ascending the Beirinyan throne, the situation had deteriorated to the point that border forces on both sides were being strengthened. Incredibly, all because of one woman's jealousy towards another, two nations, which had previously seen themselves as allies, now thought of themselves as enemies.

This was the situation Hagan I inherited when he took his seat on the Beirinyan throne.

But Asena had made one mistake — and it was a big one. She had no love for her son. More than that, she had resented the attention his father had given him, attention which she thought should have been given to her. And so, it had been left to others to raise him: a nursemaid at first, then a governess, tutors, and, of course, his father. Hagan I was his father's son but had never been his mother's.

Unlike his father, however, Hagan grew up to be a strong young man — in mind, heart, and body. One thing and one thing only he inherited from his mother. Her determination.

The Queen had no love for him, and he had none for her. He had looked on when he became old enough, seeing how Asena's self-absorption was undermining his father's reign, seeing how it was undermining Beirinya, and knowing there was nothing he could do. His father was securely trapped in her web, blind to her machinations and deaf to any criticism.

And so, in the week following his coronation, when he received a delegation from the Conclave of Priests, he listened attentively to their request, though with no outward display of his thoughts.

"The Temple of Asena is an abomination," complained the High Father, trying desperately to maintain his composure as his colleagues shuffled nervously behind him.

Beirinya's religious leader knew he was taking the biggest risk he had ever taken in the whole of his long life. The tower had been Hagan's father's crowning achievement. It had been built to proclaim his mother's glory. He would never have dared to voice his objections before King Petyr. If Mishra hadn't spoken to him in his dreams, he wouldn't be voicing them now before the son.

But Mishra was a demanding goddess. She had demanded he do so, and so he must, whatever the consequences. Either that, or put down his staff, take off his holy mantle, and resign — something no High Father had ever done.

"The tower was promised to Mishra. But then, inexplicably, and to the everlasting dismay of our Conclave, your father reneged on that promise and dedicated it to his Queen. I mean no disrespect to our beloved Queen, of course. But to put her above Mishra is an abomination . . . and a sin. The tower must be torn down." The High father halted there. He had noticed the king's right eyebrow rise when he used the word 'sin', and again at his use of the word 'must'. Perhaps he had gone too far.

"It was wrong of my father to change the dedication from Mishra to our Queen. And for that I . . . we . . . apologise."

The High Father didn't know what to say. He had expected an angry retort, at the very least. To be honest, he wouldn't have been greatly surprised if the royal executioner had been called right then and there. Criticising a king was more likely than not a fatal endeavour, even if it was the previous king.

"But we shall not tear down the tower," the King went on. "I will not humiliate my mother, no matter the folly of my father's choices. We shall right that wrong, however. We shall build a new tower, even grander, and higher, of course, than its predecessors. And it shall be Mishra's Tower. I make that promise to you right here and now. And may Mishra strike me down if I don't fulfil that sacred vow."

"Thank you, my lord," mumbled the High Father, struggling to overcome his shock. "That is indeed a most elegant and fitting response to my humble request. May Mishra guide your path now and forever more." With that, the Conclave left, every one of them sending a silent prayer of thanks to Mishra as they did so for allowing them to leave with their heads still connected to their bodies.

And so it was that in the third year of his reign, King Hagan I consecrated a new tower in Trinkolai — Mishra's Tower — ninety-two spans high. It had been built to the same specifications as its predecessor; no more, and no less. One hundred and fifty years had passed since Ravaryn II had commenced work on the first tower, and now there were five towers, and they were the wonders of their time.

In due course, Hagan's son, Torben, succeeded his father. Apart from building a fifth tower, Hagan's reign of more than fifty years had seen him restore the previous friendship between Beirinya and Verinor while at the same time augmenting and strengthening Beirinya's forts along the border with Kaj.

His purchase from Kardonia early in his reign of a large number of prime stallions and exceptional mares had not only helped boost a fledging horse-rearing industry but was also beginning to change the nature and structure of the Beirinyan army. A cavalry arm had been created and that was already beginning to impact on training, equipment, and strategy.

His commission for improvements to the harbour had proved to be equally significant, freeing up additional space for warehouses and more wharves for the great merchant traders and enabling the kingdom to begin to challenge Helidos for commercial supremacy.

All in all, on his death, he left the kingdom in a stronger place than it had ever been. Although his official title was Hagan I, in his later years, his subjects began to refer to him as Hagan the Great, and the epithet stuck. Beirinya, by this time, was at the peak of its powers.

Its kings, however, we're still obsessed with towers, and Hagan's son proved to be no more resistant to their allure than many of his predecessors.

He was a different man to his father though, having lived

long in the great ruler's shadow. In contrast to Hagan, whose robust constitution had become almost legendary, Torben suffered from constant maladies, much as his grandfather, Peter V had. So much so that, rather than follow the normal pursuits of a crown prince of House Tamear, he came to prefer the company of scholars to that of soldiers or diplomats. His father referred to him as 'my bookish son', though he loved him none the less for it.

It was no surprise then, on reflection, that his love of books drove his desire to construct a sixth tower. The palace had no real library; nothing that Torben felt deserved such a name, at least. His ascent to the throne gave him the opportunity to correct that situation.

And so, in 585 he commissioned the construction of a grand library, as a long-overdue addition to what had become over the years a truly massive palace complex. To ensure the library's prominence, he decided that a tower should be constructed above it. Nothing grand, he insisted. It should not be the highest of the towers, but nor should it be the lowest. In the end, it reached fifty-five spans above ground level. Torben filled both it and the hall below with books. In time, it became a library of some renown, the collection drawing learned scholars from all over Ilythia. Only The Great Library in Trest surpassed it. The Tower above it, though given no name at the time of its consecration, came to be known as The Book Tower. And it was the sixth great tower to rise above Trinkolai's skyline.

In 596, Torben followed his ancestors, taking his own place in the great Mausoleum of House Tamear on a hill a short distance away from the city. His son, Ravaryn IV, ascended to the throne.

Unlike many of his predecessors, Ravaryn had no particular desire to build any more towers. Fate had other plans, however, and, as with his grand-father, Hagan the Great, this time the initiative came from outside of the royal family.

It was with some surprise when, some twenty or more years into his reign, Ravaryn received a delegation from Janus, a renowned builder whose reputation was in no small part due to the exemplary work he had done around Trinkolai's foreshore for two of the great commercial houses. It was said that his achievements, both there and in Talir, had made him fabulously wealthy.

"I have a proposal for your consideration, my liege," offered Janus when he came before the king.

"Oh yes. And what might that be?" Janus was not the first to have sought the King's endorsement of what, invariably, turned out to be some altogether ill-conceived scheme. Ravaryn wondered how the man had managed to make it past the screen of royal advisors.

"If I may, my lord." Janus began to unroll the large parchment he had been holding under his arm. As it unfurled, even from where he sat, Ravaryn could see that it was a plan for a structure of some kind.

"What is that? You may approach. Show it to me."

"It is a plan for a new structure, my lord."

"It looks like a tower," the king wailed, as he realised what it was. He waved his hand in dismissal. "We already have six of those. That's quite enough I think."

Janus stepped back, as the king had bid him to, but he had no intention of giving in quite so quickly. "But none of them are like this, my lord. This is a tower like no other that has ever been built. It will stand over the six as if they were its children, huddling around its knees. It will stand one hundred and twenty-five spans high."

Ravaryn was impressed. He was very impressed. And though he didn't know it at the time, he was ensnared as well. Tower-fever was about to claim its latest victim. "The Master Builder has said that we reached the limits of our capability when we built the last two towers. They will never be surpassed."

"But I am not the Master Builder, sire. He may have reached his limit. But I have not. I will build you this tower, and it won't cost you a single copper. I will pay for it out of my own pocket. It will be my gift . . . to you, and to Beirinya. If you will let me."

The rest, of course, is history. Only a fool would refuse such an offer, and Ravaryn IV was no fool. Janus may or may not be able to build it, he thought, but his pedigree suggested the former was more likely than the latter. His existing portfolio already marked him as a builder of exceptional vision and skill. And the coffers would remain untouched. The clincher had been when Janus suggested it be called Ravaryn's Tower. Ravaryn liked that. It had a nice ring to it. It honoured not only him but several of his predecessors as well.

It was seven months before construction began. Janus was a cautious and methodical builder who believed that detailed preparations were the best guarantee of success. It was the Year of the 619th Summer of the New Age.

The work, which had begun in spring, continued all the way through summer and into autumn, and still there was no sign of the tower itself. For the design included a new audience chamber, extending the existing palace even further as a number of the previous towers had done. It was over this new chamber that the tower would rise. By the time the seasons had changed again, and the chill winds that presaged winter had begun to whistle through the winding streets that led up to the palace from the harbour, the structure of the new chamber had been completed and the tower itself had begun to take shape.

All through winter and into the following year the work when on — slowly, methodically, but inexorably upwards, ever upwards. And Janus was everywhere. It seemed that he was overseeing the positioning of every block.

For each one was important. The key to his design was building the curved walls of the tower in a series of interlocking blocks. Each block strengthening its neighbour, each block strengthening, ever strengthening, the whole. Upwards, ever upwards, like a slowly narrowing arm reaching for the sky.

Carefully, the tower began to climb. Very carefully, for not a life was lost during its construction. Yes, there were incidents, and injuries. A few were quite serious. But almost always they were due to a moment's carelessness on behalf of one of the workers. For Janus himself took no risks. Not with his team. They were as important to him as the project itself.

All through the following year, the tower inched upwards. Lifting the big blocks into position became the single-most delaying factor, especially as the tower climbed higher and higher. Not that Ravaryn ever complained. He had no cause.

Of course, he wished for it to be finished. Of course, he was impatient. Kings are ever so. But with every day, the tower inched higher, and just that little bit closer to its goal.

And so, he left Janus to do what he clearly did best.

And then, finally, on the first day of spring in 622, the job was done. Janus had built his tower — Ravaryn's Tower — and the King was happy, as were his people.

Trinkolai's seven towers were the wonder of their time. How could anyone have thought that six would be sufficient? The seven were marvellous. Both Beirinya and Trinkolai's fame exceeded all bounds. As if that weren't enough, the year 622 marked two hundred and fifty years since construction of the very first tower had commenced. In celebration, Ravaryn IV hosted a fair which lasted for a whole cycle of the moon. The streets ran with wine and ale. There had never been a better time to be a Trinkolite.

In time, Torben II succeeded Ravaryn IV, and he, in turn, was succeeded by his son — Hagan II. Both of their reigns were relatively uneventful, although the kingdom continued to prosper. The stimulus their illustrious ancestor, Hagan the Great, had given to horse-rearing, in particular, began to pay huge dividends, with Beirinyan studs finally overtaking their Kardonian competitors as the breeders of the finest horses in all the land. Beirinyan Swifts now commanded huge prices and there was barely an equine competition that wasn't won off the back of one of these superb steeds. Breeding mares were almost worth their weight in gold, such was their dominance in the field.

And so it was, during the reign of Hagan II, that a significant anniversary began to approach.

The year 662 would mark four hundred years since their ancestor, Ravaryn I, had overthrown Jamal III and been crowned as King of Beirinya, a position House Tamear had filled ever since. Hagan II was the thirteenth Tamearan ruler in unbroken succession since that time.

The king decided that nothing less than grandest of all celebrations would suffice to mark such a milestone and, by 661, the whole kingdom was abuzz with expectation. Hagan II had let it be known that 662 would mark the beginning of a whole year of festivities, the like of which the populace would never have seen before. There was barely a merchant who hadn't been contracted to contribute their wares to some aspect of what promised to be a year of great carousing and merry-making.

But something was missing. The various fairs, festivals, fetes, pageants, carnivals, and jamborees would certainly adorn an unprecedented commemoration of House Tamear's four hundred years of rule, but the celebrations lacked a signature event.

Until, that is, Hagan II turned his gaze skywards one day and realised that the obvious candidate had been staring him in the face the whole of his life. An eighth tower would be the crowning event. Its consecration, on the very first day of the new year, would be the perfect event to herald the year of celebrations which would follow.

But there was just under a year to go. There would be no time to waste. At least one of the previous towers had taken nearly three years to complete. The first, however, Hagan II remembered, had been built in less than a year, and Beirinyan builders were by now well-versed in how to construct these grand structures. They would simply be repeating what previous Beirinyan builders had done before them. No expense would be spared. It could be done. It would be done.

And so it was that work began on the eighth great tower to adorn the royal palace in Trinkolai.

Within only a few months, the foundations were complete and the tower itself began to rise. The Master Builder of the day had quickly overcome his doubts and had risen to the challenge. His days were long, as were those of his teams, but nothing was allowed to hinder progress. While the builder resigned himself to only a few hours sleep each day, he called upon the resources Hagan II had promised and soon had three teams hard at work. They operated in rotating shifts, ensuring that the workers were always fresh. A host of lanterns were brought in once the sun had set. Teams of cooks, medicants and all manner of other assistants saw to the workers' every need. Visitors to the Beirinyan capital marvelled at the expertise and ingenuity of the local craftsman. They truly did know how to build towers in Beirinya.

A small hiccup occurred with only two cycles of the moon left until the scheduled day for completion. The rapidity of the construction had led to a small amount of instability in the structure as the tower approached its planned zenith. In a moment of inspiration, the Master Builder devised an ingenious solution.

Rather than stone, the final five spans that would take it just that little bit higher than the previous tower would be crafted in curved metal plates. They would be securely bolted to the great blocks already in place. It would be even stronger than continuing with stone. It would also enable a viewing platform to adorn the top. The winding internal staircase would open on to a metal platform, with a railing all the way around, enabling up to twenty or so people to stand at the very top of the structure. From there they would have an unprecedented view across the Beirinyan capital. On the day of its consecration, while invited guests would throng in the great courtyard at the tower's base, those at the top would be able to marvel at the fleet of great merchant ships which was due to assemble in the harbour as yet another aspect of the celebrations.

The great day arrived and everything was complete. The structure was sound and, if anything, the view from its apex was even better than the Master Builder had anticipated. Though the weather was not what the king had hoped for, with dark clouds forming to the north, and the occasional squall of rain dampening the roofs of the great marquees which had been set up for the occasion, Hagan II realised that there were some things that no number of royal decrees could right.

At the appointed hour, Hagan and the royal family assembled. The tower had been consecrated and given its official name — the Tamearan Tower — in honour of their house. The whole family then ascended to the viewing platform, led by Hagan II and his wife, the Queen, along with their three children. After them, came his sister, with her husband and her two young boys. His aunt was also there, with her family, as were several more distant relatives. All in all, twenty-three members of House Tamear squeezed together on the viewing platform.

Below them, in the courtyard, the revellers were in full song. From where he stood, atop their grandest monument, the king could make out the words of the Beirinyan national song rising up from the broiling mass of courtiers and select visitors below, despite the occasional boom of thunder as black clouds began to roll in over the city.

He turned towards his queen, feeling his heart swelling with pride at their achievement, when, all of a sudden, with a blinding flash and a deafening crack of thunder, his world turned upside down. Within a fraction of a heartbeat, a fearsome bolt of lightning had struck the metal plates on the side of the tower and the top of the Tamearan Tower had burst into a thousand pieces. Huge twisted and blackened metal plates plunged toward the stunned crowd milling around the tower's base, accompanied by bloodied body parts and a deadly deluge of stone. Blocks of every shape and size, from some as big as a carriage down to others that could have been mistaken for hailstones, rained down on the terrified onlookers. There was no chance for anyone to seek shelter.

After a few minutes, the deadly deluge finally came to a halt. The shower of gruesome debris was replaced by a steady drizzle of rain. The courtyard was a horrifying scene of death and destruction. In many ways, the royal entourage atop the metal viewing platform had been the lucky ones. For them, the bolt would have bought an instantaneous death. The crowd below were less fortunate. Some were crushed by huge blocks of stone, or sheared in two by one of the huge metal plates. From the groans and screams rising above the patter of the rain, many others had survived, for the moment at least, but had suffered terrible injuries.

It took several minutes before anyone moved to help them, so stunned were those who had watched on in horror from safer vantage points. It took much longer still for the wailing and the screaming to subside. It seemed to go on forever. Many were still replaying the memory of the horrific event over and over again in their minds.

The incident was, and remains to this date, the greatest calamity that had ever befallen the kingdom.

House Tamear no longer existed, unless you count two young sisters, distant cousins of the king, who were too sick to attend the event. They had remained in their home, tucked up safely in their beds and attended by their governess, while their parents went off to join the royal entourage.

A further one hundred and seventy-nine members of the royal court, who had been in the throng in the courtyard, would never return to their homes. More than thirty-five more courtiers were taken to the houses of healing. Eight of these did not survive the night. For the next several days, it seemed there was an endless procession of funeral cortèges winding their ways out of the city and up to the mausoleums of all the great houses in the nearby hills.

Perhaps as many as thirty or forty attendants and guards had also perished, though no precise records were kept of fatalities and injuries outside of the nobility. Their burials were nowhere near as ostentatious as those of the rich, but proved their equal in attendant mourners.

Within days, Altin, from House Harfan, was crowned king. With two notable exceptions — the two young girls who had survived the tragedy — House Tamear took no further part in the history of Beirinya.

One of Altin's first decrees was a ban on any written record of the calamitous event. Though the kingdom's grief knew no bounds, their shame at its cause — the folly of overweening pride — was equally great. Although the memory of such an occurrence could not possibly be expunged from memory, or from oral history, Beirinya nonetheless did its best to wipe any written record of the day from its history.

No further towers were ever built in Trinkolai — of any kind. Seven were deemed to be more than enough.

And yet despite what happened on that most calamitous of days, despite the ultimate tragedy 'tower-fever' had eventually engendered, the Seven Towers of Trinkolai are still to this day the single-most admired architectural wonders in all of Ilythia.

THE MAN WITH THE WRONG SHADOW

O f all the unusual things about Tanis, the perplexing nature of his shadow is, I think, the most intriguing — it leans towards the sun rather than away from it! Before I elaborate on that seemingly impossible observation, however, I need to go back to the beginning. You will see then why I was drawn to him right from the start. You will also see, I hope, why I have arrived at the decision I have.

It all began back in July, at the introductory lecture for Greek Mythology, one of my second semester papers here at the University of Otago. The lecture had barely begun when I suddenly became conscious of the man seated next to me. My focus at that point had been on the lecturer and the handout he had passed around before he commenced talking. I soon found, however, that my neighbour was going to be one I wished had seated himself elsewhere.

Right from the beginning I could see that he was a very nervous fellow. He was constantly fidgeting and sighing and generally carrying on in a most distracting manner, making it almost impossible for me to maintain my focus on what the lecturer had to say. Fortunately, he settled down about half-way through the presentation, just as I was on the verge of getting up and moving to another seat. Then, as we got up to leave, I heard him mutter, almost sotto voice, "Why dress it up as myth unless you've got something to hide?"

"Sorry?" I responded after a few moments, not sure what he meant, or if he was speaking to me rather than to himself, as I had first thought.

"I just don't know why they persist in dressing this stuff up as myths," he exclaimed earnestly, turning and looking at me as we walked out into the hall. "Am I the only one who sees through that?"

"What do you mean?"

Well, those must have been the magic words. Maybe I was just in the wrong place at the wrong time. Perhaps I just have one of those faces that makes people want to pour out their deepest secrets to a total stranger. Five minutes later, we were sitting down together, me nursing a flat white and him with a long black, at Cafe Albany in the ISB Link. That was when the real crazy stuff started pouring out.

His name was Tanis, he said. No first name, or was it no surname? Just Tanis. He was tall, with dark, black, wavy hair of medium length. It looked like it hadn't been cut for some time, a bit straggly around the edges and starting to come down over his ears just a tad. He had a lean frame that was, at the same time, noticeably muscular. Not in any overt, body-building type way. He was just clearly very fit. He looked to be around forty or so, though I later found out that this was a very, very, long way off the mark of what he claimed!

As for what he had to say: he claimed to have come here, that is to 'our world', from another world altogether – from Ilythia, as he called it.

I guess you would have got up and left at that point, perhaps with some excuse that you had forgotten you needed to be elsewhere, perhaps without bothering with an excuse at all, just collected your belongings and got the hell out of there as fast as you could. I didn't.

Too stunned to move a muscle, my mouth agape and my tongue stuck to the roof of my mouth. I couldn't speak, so I just let him go on. And go on he did, as if he had some long-withheld need to get it all out, to tell someone about his 'situation', as he called it.

He came here through a 'portal', he told me, which he himself created by means of a spell he had cast back in Ilythia. He was a wizard, of course, because only wizards can cast spells!

He wasn't really a student at the university, he confessed. His intention was to just 'sit in' on a number of papers which he found of particular interest. Greek Mythology wasn't the only one. He was also interested in lectures on Quantum and Thermal Physics as well as Quantum, Atomic and Particle Physics.

In the case of Greek Mythology, he said that he suspected the so-called myths weren't myths at all. He believed they may be history of an earlier time, one which to him seemed to have strong synergies with his own world, with Ilythia, that is.

He told me that ours wasn't the world he had thought he would be travelling to. He arrived in the University of Otago Clocktower Building. In a small alcove in the tower, directly behind the clock itself, to be more precise. Somehow, he had taken a wrong turn, only, this was the mother of all wrong turns.

Thus far, he told me, he had been unable to cast the spell to get home again. Whether that was because magic wasn't possible here, or because the requirements for casting the spell differed here in some way he had not yet been able to discern, he was unsure. The result, however, was the same. He was 'trapped' here. Trapped in Dunedin! He didn't seem to find it at all amusing when I told him many younger Dunedinites felt the same!

"I guess you'd never know it from how I must look now,

but I was a person of great importance in Ilythia, you know," he went on.

He paused then and gazed out the window with a wistful look. All the while I just sat there, rooted to the spot, still with no idea how to respond . . . and not even sure I wanted to. Perhaps he was an actor, I thought, and he was rehearsing a role, trying his lines out on me to gauge my response. Or maybe it was a story he was intending to write. A brief nod was all I could manage.

"I tired of that role eventually," he went on. "Well . . . wouldn't anyone? I'd done it for a few centuries by then."

I almost choked on a mouthful of coffee at that. "Mmmmm," I recovered, trying desperately to keep a straight face as I spoke. "That *is* a long time, isn't it?"

"I already knew how to use the Spell of Portal to move around Ilythia," he went on, "but I began to think more and more about the possibility of exploring other worlds."

One of the key elements that enabled him to cast such a powerful spell as the Spell of Portal, he told me, was a crystal he had brought with him from Ilythia.

The object he placed on the table in front of me then looked, at first, like a large, black, quartz crystal, about as big as a cigar, only shorter, and considerably thicker. When I picked it up to examine it, however, I immediately sensed that this was not a normal crystal. It was warm in my hand, for one thing, but then only a moment or two later it felt quite cool, almost chill, then moments later it was warm again. The temperature seemed to be pulsating, slowly moving from warm to chill and back again, in a continuous cycle.

Looking closely, I found its appearance was equally disturbing. Rather than a static piece of crystal, the inside of it seemed to be continuously seething, as if it was full of smoke, or some gelatinous liquid that was slowly swirling about creating random and bizarre patterns.

At that point, my interest in Tanis' story, which had already shifted from awkward disdain to fascination, began to shift, to change to one of wonder. I still didn't think for a moment that what he had told me was true, but . . . no, I tell a lie, a very small part of me did start to wonder if it could at all be possible. I quickly suppressed the thought, feeling foolish for even considering such a thing.

But what a hoax, what detail and conviction his story held. And this crystal, where could you possibly acquire such a thing?

At that point, to my dismay, I realised I had to leave. Though the temptation to stay and listen to more of his story was almost overwhelming, I had another class to go to and several personal matters to attend to before the shops shut. And so, I hastily departed.

As I scurried off across the campus on my way to my next lecture, and indeed, over the course of the next twenty-four hours until I caught up with him again, I found it almost impossible to stop thinking about Tanis and his story. I wondered at why I had so quickly become obsessed with his tale, until I realised. It was because I could see that *he* believed it. True or not, it had become *his* reality. He truly was caught in a trap. Whether it was a physical one, or a mental one, remained to be seen, but he was caught, nonetheless.

How must he feel, I wondered at the time? The fall from being the most important person in his world to being one of the most insignificant, trapped here in a small town in one of the southernmost reaches of habitable space on our planet would break almost anyone. Even if it weren't true, if *he* believed it, that would be enough to breed despair the likes of which I could only begin to imagine.

When we met again the next day at a café over on Cumberland Street, I suggested we sit outside. It was a mild day and, though I felt guilty at the thought, I realised I didn't want others to hear our conversation. I knew I would be embarrassed if they did so. Even though they wouldn't know I was actually entertaining the thought that there might be something to his story, I was embarrassed at the fact that I was.

The best way to dispel such thoughts, I concluded, would be to find the flaw in his story, the chink in his armour. And so, I came armed with questions. Once the waitress had brought out our coffees, I began to probe his story more closely.

"So, what did you do when you first arrived here?" I asked him. "How have you managed to survive in what must be a very strange world indeed to you?" And with that he was off and running again. It was as if his story from the previous day had been paused and I had just hit the Start Button again.

"As you can imagine," he began, in the same earnest manner he had exhibited the day before, "it took me some time to find my feet. For the first few days, I just wandered around in a daze. Cars were the first things I encountered which really made me wonder what I had got myself into. The speed of the things, and all of that metal, not to mention how in the world they were moving, what force was propelling them forward. Then, once I'd got over that, I found my way down to the harbour, and the sight of the huge metal ships there was almost equally unbelievable.

"It took me some days before I got my head around the fact that I truly was in a different world, so I shouldn't be surprised to find it was one where things were so utterly different to my own. I'd known there would be differences, of course, but I hadn't considered they would be on such a vast scale.

"Money, of course, quickly became a problem. I found what I now understand is the main street, with all those vast shops, more I think in that one place than there are in all of Ilythia, and so I also found toilets and access to water, freely available to anyone who wanted it. Quite amazing!

"But food was a real problem. I went hungry for the first

two days. To my shame, in my desperation, I resorted to stealing some fruit. But I knew that couldn't go on. The last thing I wanted was for the Sheriff or the Town Guard to clap me in irons. Then I came across a bank. I went in and asked some of the people there if I could exchange the gold coins I had brought with me from Ilythia for some of the local currency. To my surprise, they didn't want anything to do with them. The woman I spoke to was helpful, nonetheless, and she pointed me in the direction of what she called a coin collector. Up in Church Street, she said.

"I eventually found my way there and got what I now understand must have been a very good deal. He took some time examining my twenty crowns and seemed to be very excited, though he was clearly trying not to show it. He made me an offer of a few thousand dollars. I could tell from his reaction, however, that they must have been worth more than he was saying. Well, I know how to haggle. In the end I got quite a lot more for them.

"That solved my money problems, at least for quite some time, but I still had nowhere to stay. I spent several nights under some shrubs in a big, wooded area up on the hill behind the town. I also found a shop that sold used clothing incredibly cheaply, at least in comparison to the prices for similar attire in the shops in the main street. The man who served me there was very kind. He asked me if I was 'sleeping rough'. I didn't know what that meant so I just nodded. Then he told me about what he called a 'soup kitchen', where homeless people like me could get a simple meal once a day.

"I had bought a bag as well, and some blankets and other necessities. Carrying all that around was a problem, however. Then I stumbled on a vast shop which seemed to sell almost every food you could imagine, and much more besides. 'New World' it was called. It was the name that first drew my attention, of course. I found a trolley there which I could use to carry all of my belongings in. A 'trundle' I think it is called, though as no one else was using one once they left that shop, I guessed that they weren't meant to be used in that way.

"What really turned things around for me, however, was when, after several days of wandering, I saw a sign on a house in George Street which said, 'Room for Rent'. It was very expensive by my reckoning, but it came with some simple items of furniture already there, including a bed. As I had enough money from the sale of my coins, I took it straight away, and that's where I've been ever since. I have a roof over my head now, and enough money for food and the like, as long as I'm frugal. I know that it won't last forever, but I still have some more coins to sell if what I have runs out.

"I'm hopeful that won't be the case. Just last week I got myself a job." At this, Tanis beamed as if he had won the lottery. "It's just servant-class work," he went on. "Working for a business that has the contract for cleaning the city's libraries, including those here at the university. I didn't even know such places existed here until I got that job.

"But the best thing is that now I'm confident I can find out how to cast the spell here in Earth. There must be something in all those books that will help me to understand what I need to do. I have started to research everything I can find out about magic."

And so his story went on. We were on to our second cup of coffee by now, and still he seemed to have every nook and cranny of his tale covered. If there was a gap somewhere, it was clearly going to be hard to find.

"But what about language," I asked nonchalantly, trying not to betray the importance of the question. I watched him very closely as I explained what I meant, for I was sure I had him here. He couldn't possibly explain how he came here from another world where they just happen to speak Shakespeare's English. "You must use a different language to what we speak here back in Ilythia," I said. "How is it that you can speak English so fluently?"

"That's the real beauty of the variation of the Spell of Portal I used," he responded without a moment's hesitation. "It has a subsidiary spell, a translation spell, embedded within it. Whoever goes through the portal can understand whatever language he or she encounters in any new world they enter. Similarly, without even realising it, they speak in the language of that world. Whatever language I would have encountered here, I would have understood it, and the inhabitants would have understood me. Some of the idioms don't translate well, but that's all."

"Wow," I said, taken aback by the speed of his answer. He must have prepared for that question. I wasn't done yet, however. "So, that waitress who served us, from her accent, my guess is that she's a tourist. If I asked her to say something to you in her native tongue, you would understand it and be able to speak back to her the same."

"Yes. I can't see why not. Don't you believe me? Let's try it."

"Okay." I waited a few moments until I could get the waitress' attention with a wave. She came out to serve us once she had finished at one of the tables inside. "Hello," I began, with a smile. "My name is Peter, and this is Tanis. I couldn't help but notice that you have quite a strong accent. Is that something European? Are you a tourist here?"

"I am," she replied with a broad grin. "I am from Hungary to here."

"Cool. Are you enjoying your trip to New Zealand?"

"I love it," she responded with enthusiasm. "This is a beautiful country. You are very lucky to be living here."

"Thank you. I've never heard anyone speak Hungarian. Could you say something to my friend here in Hungarian?"

"Sure. Szia. A barátja próbál beszélgetni velem, vagy ő csak baráti?"

Tanis smiled back at her, then responded without a moment's hesitation. "Szia. Ő csak barátságos. Ne is törődj vele."

With that, the waitress turned and smiled at me, then went

back inside to serve some of the other customers. I just sat there grinning back at Tanis, too surprised to even begin to know what to say in response to what had just happened. I'd never been to Hungary, but I had heard that Hungarian, along with Finnish, were two of the most difficult of all European languages to learn.

"And there you see why I am so confident that there is a way for me to cast the Spell of Portal again," said Tanis, interrupting my thoughts. "The translation spell that sat within the parent portal spell is still working. Magic *is* possible here in Earth . . .'

"*On* Earth. We say, 'on Earth', not 'in Earth'."

"Oh! Okay. Magic is possible here *on* Earth. I just have to find the right catalyst here for the Spell of Portal."

Over the next few months, I ran into him again on campus a number of times, and each time he would update me on how his research was coming along into how to cast his spell and move on from 'this world'.

One thing was clear, he knew how to research! He had been to all of the public libraries: the Dunedin City Library, the Waikouaiti Library, the Blueskin Bay Library, the Port Chalmers Library, even the Mosgiel Library. He had even learnt how to go online in some of those places and had begun to search the Internet. He was no fool, however, and had quickly absorbed the importance of treating the latter with caution. Like any good researcher, he understood the need to consider the reliability of sources.

He had also checked out all of the university libraries. His favourites were the Central Library, the Hocken, and the Science Library over in Science III.

At one stage, he apparently became quite excited when he had read about ley lines. He understood that many reputable scholars dismissed this as pseudoscientific nonsense, but he was having none of that. The theory behind them aligned almost perfectly with his worldview. More than that, he thought they may be one of the key ingredients to enabling magic in our world.

"Magic, that is, real magic, not magician's tricks," he told me fervently, "has been suppressed in your world. Science is king, and magic doesn't fit with your scientists' views of how the world works. They can't measure it, nor can they explain it. Why, I read about how, in what they call the Middle Ages, they burnt people who practised it at the stake. How abominable!

"You know, this world of yours . . . there seems to be a popular belief that it is quite sophisticated and advanced. Of course, in many ways it is. Just look at that mobile phone of yours. From what I understand of its capabilities . . . well, let's just say that I can't even begin to fathom how all that could be possible.

"But magic? What do they call its adherents? 'Fringe dwellers', 'loonies'? Your society actively marginalises such people and such beliefs. Is it any wonder it has been driven underground?"

As for ley lines, Tanis was convinced there was one running underneath the university, and that it was 'humped'. That is, it came closer to the surface at some points, and was therefore more powerful in those places than at others. He believed that one of these points was under the Clocktower Building. He was certain it was that which had led to his Spell of Portal, once it had erroneously found this world, locating its terminus at that point.

Unfortunately, shortly after his arrival, the University began some maintenance work on the tower. Earthquake strengthening! Clearly that was going to take some time. And so, he had two choices: wait until that work was done, assuming he could resolve whatever other requirements there were for casting the spell here, or find another equally auspicious location.

A few weeks after that, I met him again. At a coffee shop, of course. He just couldn't get enough of the stuff. At least he was broadening his addictions, however, for by that time he had also discovered chocolate. He must have spent the first half hour or so going on and on about the different types he'd been able to find. Of all of them, Whittakers was his favourite. He was, of course, given his admiration for the substance, aghast at the decision by Cadbury to close their factory here in Dunedin. He told me that when he first heard there was a place called Cadbury World, his immediate reaction was 'I want to go to that world!'

Eventually, I managed to steer the conversation away from chocolate and back to his research. It was then that he told me he'd located what he believed was a second 'hump' in the ley line that ran beneath the university campus. It was in Scott Shand House. What's more, he had reconnoitred the building and there was a small storage room there which should be ideal for his purposes. Now, all he had to do was identify the right catalyst for casting his spell here on Earth.

I tell you; those talks I had with Tanis, putting aside the great coffee — he had a knack for finding all of the very best coffee shops in Dunedin — were nothing if not entertaining.

For all the seriousness of his obsession, there was a funny side to him at times too. On one occasion, he told me that he had discovered movies. He'd got himself a cheap, second-hand 'television set', as he called it, and a second-hand DVD player, then convinced one of his neighbours to help him get it all working. Then he had gone out and splurged on a half dozen or more DVDs — the Lord of the Rings trilogy and all of The Hobbit movies. He loved them!

On Saturdays, he told me, he would go down to the Farmers' Market at the train station and buy some Elderberry wine, or whatever similar beverage he could find. And then, on Saturday night, he would stock up on chocolate and other junk food, and sit down to binge watch the Lord of the Rings. All three movies. *Every* Saturday night.

Talk about an addict! I dreaded the thought of what might happen if anyone ever introduced him to hard drugs.

I told him I would lend him my DVD of the first Narnia movie: The Lion, the Witch and the Wardrobe. I suspected he would identify with the situation those children got themselves into. If only it would be as simple for him as stepping into a wardrobe to get back home!

Another amusing story he told me, though from his perspective it was a serious endeavour and one potentially full of great promise, was the letter he wrote to Elon Musk. He had read a number of stories about the entrepreneur and then had researched him quite thoroughly. He was quite taken, in particular, by Musk's claim that he saw the Mars project as a way of escaping from what he saw as a doomed planet. Tanis decided to write to Mr. Musk. And he did.

He told me he had explained his own plight to Mr. Musk quite frankly and in some detail. He also told him that, from what he had seen in his brief time here, and what he understood of the dramatic changes which were occurring in terms of our climate, he could only agree with Musk's appraisal of mankind's likely imminent demise. He went on to explain that he could offer Mr. Musk a safer and much quicker exit strategy than his Mars project could, namely, the Spell of Portal. He offered to take Musk with him when he left. All he needed in exchange was a few million dollars to hire a team of researchers to help him solve the riddle of how to re-cast it here on Earth. With those kinds of resources, he had no doubt that he would have the problem solved within a month or two, if not earlier.

At the time of telling me all of this, he had not yet received a reply from Musk's office. He had high hopes for its success, however.

I didn't want to rain on his parade but tried to soften the likely outcome by suggesting that it might take quite a long time before he got a reply, if ever. I told him my guess was that Elon Musk received scores, if not hundreds of business proposals every week. He would no doubt be quite ruthless in determining which ones he might respond to. I didn't tell him what I really thought — that someone in Musk's office would have had a quiet chuckle over the letter before dispatching it to the wastepaper basket.

I now have no shame in revealing that, having given a

great deal of thought to the matter and, as you can see from my notes above, having examined Tanis' story at some length, my belief is that he might very well be telling the truth — as ridiculous as that may sound.

Putting aside the complexity and the watertight detail of his story, there are a number of points which, though each compelling in its own way, together have convinced me.

I managed to track down the coins he sold shortly after his arrival. I took careful note of where he said he had sold them and then, one day, went there myself. I told the proprietor I had heard he had purchased a number of very rare if not unique gold coins and that I was interested in buying them from him.

The proprietor had no difficulty with that at all. It is, after all, what he does. The outcome was that I was able to buy them back from him, though at a hefty mark-up from the amount Tanis said he had received for them. I could afford it, and that enabled me to examine them quite closely.

The coin dealer indicated his belief, confirmed by a very experienced colleague, was that they are most probably of middle eastern origin. Pre-Roman definitely, and perhaps from as far back at the Hittite empire, or from thereabouts. They could find no record of anything similar at all, however, so that was only their best guess.

A jeweller friend of mine subsequently confirmed they are certainly of gold, though the metal's signature is like none he has ever seen before. The gold content alone ensured they are worth a considerable sum, as they are quite large coins, not at all like the tiny Aureus, the gold coin during the days of the Roman Empire.

The crystal is the second item which has influenced me, though it is hard to explain in words, unless you have seen it yourself, as I have, how 'alien' it obviously is. I described it to one of the professors from the Department of Geology at the university and he assured me that it must have been a trick of the light. No rock, or crystal, or any other similar object, he said, could possibly behave in the way I had described.

Then there was the matter of Tanis' ability to speak other languages quite fluently. This really tipped the balance in favour of the verisimilitude of his story as far as I was concerned. I only had the chance to test him on this twice. The first was that time with the Hungarian waitress which I outlined above. There was also a second and similar occasion that really got me thinking. I shouted Tanis to a meal in a Thai restaurant one night, thinking that would be a real treat for him, only for him to end up in a long conversation in Thai with the owner while I was paying the bill. Once again, I was dumbfounded at his apparent fluency in what can't be a commonly known language.

But the final straw, the clincher, so to speak, especially coming on top of everything else, was his shadow. That was one of the most curious things of all.

No, it was more than that. It sent a chill down my spine

the first time I saw it, though Tanis took great pains to conceal it. Why I still do not know. It was only much later, after I had become aware of his shadow, that I realised he spent most of his daylight hours inside, especially on sunny days, in the library, doing his research, venturing out and, certainly, meeting me, only at midday or in the late evening, after dusk.

His shadow, bizarrely, leaned towards the sun, not away from it!

It was almost as if it was still being cast by the sun of another world, not this one. That was the only explanation I could come up with when I thought about it later. I never challenged him about it. I'm not really sure why that was, though I suspect now I was in denial. I knew deep down that this was a clincher, and I wasn't ready to face up to that.

I have overcome that resistance now. I was watching *Sherlock* on TV on Tuesday night. You know, the recent version, the one with Benedict Cumberbatch. He used that famous saying: 'Once you eliminate the impossible, whatever remains, no matter how improbable, must be the truth'. It was at that point that I realised: I believe Tanis.

Perhaps there is more to it than that. I know that deep down the real reason might be simply that I *want* to believe him, that I *want* to believe there are other worlds than our own. It makes no difference why, however. I believe him.

My mind is incessantly whirling, and I can feel my heart hammering against my chest. Such exciting news! Tanis has found the way to cast the Spell of Portal. He has even tested it. He did so in the early hours of this very morning, and I have only just come back from catching up with his news. In the end, he said, it was simply a matter of being in the right place *and* at the right time. In this case, that means where the ley lines are the strongest — he has known for some time that is in Scott Shand House — *and* at dawn. I have no idea why dawn is a factor in the matter, but he is brimming over with excitement too. He intends to spend the day packing the things he wants to take with him. He means to go without delay. At dawn tomorrow.

I have decided to go with him!

I've arranged to meet him later this evening at his rented accommodation. We'll go over to Scott Shand House early tomorrow, while most of the city is still asleep, and then we'll be off, just as the sun rises. Today will be my last full day in Dunedin!

You mustn't think this a hasty decision. I have been mulling it over for some time and have had many a sleepless night as a consequence. I haven't said anything to anyone other than Tanis, mainly because I wasn't actually sure of what I would do. Until now. Tanis' latest news has helped clarify everything for me.

It was Tanis who put the idea into my head. Well . . . that isn't totally true. I had wondered what I would do if he pulled it off, whether I would want to go with him, if he would have me. I wasn't game to ask him, though. I was afraid he would laugh at me. Then, a few days ago, he put the proposal to me. I was quite surprised, especially at how eager he was to have a companion on his grand adventure. I had thought him a confirmed loner.

And so, it is done and decided. Just like that.

For the sake of those who love me and, I trust, will miss me, and so they will know what has happened to me, I will leave a printout on my mantlepiece of this record I have kept of Tanis' brief sojourn here in our world.

If his attempt at casting the spell fails, I will be disappointed. There will be nothing for it then but to return to my home and complete the record accordingly.

But if it succeeds, as I am quite confident now that it will? Well, in that case, 'Farewell'. I can only hope that you will understand why the chance being offered, to explore another world, is just too fantastic, and too irresistible, to pass up. Neil Armstrong, eat your heart out. You only went to the moon.

Wish me well.

Signed - Peter _____, 22 February 2019

Editor's Addendum

The following item appeared in several newspapers across New Zealand on the 17th March this year:

'New Zealand Police have reported a strange finding inside a flat in North Dunedin.

Police responded to a call on the morning of the 23rd February this year. On arrival at the scene, police officers located the body of a long-term Dunedin resident, Mr. Peter _____, a student at the University of Otago.

A police spokesman has advised that Mr. _____ appeared to have died of as yet unknown causes sometime on the night of 22nd February. Police are treating their inquiries as a homicide investigation.

Unconfirmed sources have informed this reporter that a quantity of blood had been taken from the body of Mr. _____. Residue of a substance which has been confirmed by analysts as blood of the deceased was apparently found in both a bowl and a small brazier inside the room, along with small quantities of a mixture of uncommon and rare herbs and plants. Speculation is that some sort of ritual or ceremony was conducted in the room, utilising the blood taken from the victim, along with some of the herbs and other plant material. New Zealand Police have refused to comment on this speculation.

New Zealand Police have advised, however, that the current tenant of the flat in question, a Mr. Tanis, has not been located. The bedroom where Mr. _____'s body was found was locked from the inside, as was the one window. Police have not been able to locate any other means of entry or exit from the room other than through the window or the door.

Police believe that the bulk of Mr. Tanis' belongings are also missing. The only objects left behind in the flat were some DVDs and a rather considerable collection of books, primarily on subjects related to black magic, physics, and chemistry, and almost all 'borrowed' from various libraries around the town.

The police spokesman has confirmed that there were signs of a struggle within the room.

Police have requested that anyone knowing the whereabouts of Mr. Tanis, or with any information that may be relevant to this case, should contact the Crimestoppers Hotline on _____.'

THE INTERVIEW

It was only after his death that Peter Maynard changed. While ever he walked this earth, he had been a man who was, almost universally, well-liked, and much-admired. He had his faults, of course, and a few enemies, as would anyone who spent more than six decades living amongst his fellows, but, for the most part, his ruddy complexion and ever-cheerful disposition endeared him to all who crossed his path. Once he passed over, however, those rosy cheeks finally paled, that ever-present smile fled, displaced by a permanent frown, and even his renowned positive attitude took a complete u-turn.

They say that, for some, 'death becomes them'. Well, I've never met one, and certainly Peter was not a member of that club. And I'm not just talking about those first few hours, when, like everyone who wakes up dead, he had no idea he was no longer amongst the living. Once he accepted that he wasn't dreaming, and that the reason no-one could see him, hear him, or touch him, was because he had passed over, that's when he really got angry. And then he just stayed that way.

At first, a layer of depression masked his anger. Walking the streets of Dunedin, he found the city covered in what seemed to be a shroud of thin mist, like a fog on a summer morn that had begun to clear but then, for some inexplicable reason, got stuck and couldn't completely dissipate. It gave the place an ethereal appearance which only served to heighten his already sombre mood. It was also curiously chilly given the time of year. It was only February. He'd been swimming down at Brighton barely a week before.

The cold seemed to seep right into his bones, and he soon found himself wishing they'd clothed his corpse in something other than a lightweight summer suit, even if it was the one he always wore to funerals — how annoyingly ironic! His black winter coat and corduroy trousers would have been more suitable for conditions like those he was experiencing. Not that it seemed to be bothering anyone else. Many of the young women he encountered were flouncing about in short skirts and skimpy tops and some of the lads were wearing tee-shirts. He felt envious, and not just at their vitality. He seemed to be the only one feeling a need to keep warm.

Until, that is, he saw the old woman standing outside the entrance to Knox Church. She had on just the kind of big winter coat he could have done with for these kinds of conditions. But there was something else about her too. While everyone else seemed just that little bit blurred, a bit out of focus in some way, as if he was seeing them through someone else's glasses, she was as clear as a freshly washed windowpane; and she looked straight at him when he crossed Pitt and turned the corner into George Street. She could see him!

All of a sudden, he realised why. She must be dead too. That's why she seemed so alive. Wherever he was — and I don't mean Dunedin, I mean this plane of existence, or otherworld, or wherever it was that he was — she was there too. She even greeted him when he approached her. It was his first interaction with anyone since he had died, not counting, of course, all the people he'd tried to talk to on the way down to the city, but who'd either ignored him, or walked straight on through him, or both.

"Hello," he exclaimed, relieved to find he wasn't alone after all. "What's going on here? Where are we?"

"Hi there. I'm Marge — thanks for askin'. This is George Street. You're in Dunedin. What's wrong? You just wake up or somethin'?"

"I sure did. Sorry Marge. I'm Peter. I'm . . . I'm a bit at sixes and sevens. I'm just not where I expected to be. Actually, to be honest, I didn't expect anything at all. I didn't even know I was about to die, though I assume that's what must have happened. This black suit sort of gives it way, I guess. That, and the fact that no one can see me . . . and people keep walking right through me. It's very annoying."

"Don't worry, Peter. You'll get used to it. WhereeverWeAreGoing must be havin' a busy day."

"Sorry?"

"WhereverWeAreGoing — that's what we call the place we are goin' on to eventually. Right now, you're in WhereverWeAre and you've come from WhereverWeWere."

"What? Who invented those silly names? They're not exactly very poetic, are they? Isn't this the AfterLife? Isn't that where we are?"

"You can call it that if you like. In fact, you can call it anythin' you want to for all I care. But you'll find they're the 'silly' names the rest of us use."

"Us? Are there more of us? You're the only other one I've seen."

"Oh yeh, there're a few of us 'round the place. I saw young Nathan goin' into the mall on my way up here. And there's Marie, of course. She's always up at the Octagon. There's a few. You hang 'round long enough, you'll get to meet 'em all. Unless you get a job."

"But why are we here? Why haven't we gone on to WhereverWeAreGoing? Is that what you called it?"

"Yeh. There you go. You got it. Well . . . as I said, they must be busy up there at the moment. It happens. Not too often, thankfully, or there'd be a lot more of us down here. As to why? Who can say? Maybe there's a war goin' on somewhere. There's always one of those happenin' somewhere in the world. Right? From what I understand, the Arrivals people get pretty busy then. Too many people dyin' at once. They get overwhelmed sometimes. Creates a backlog, you see? Then some of us have to wait a bit — 'til we can get back in the queue. That's what Nettie says, anyway. Me? I just think it's a software glitch. You know, like in that movie, The Matrix?"

At that, Peter was stumped. Was she having him on? Surely the AfterLife didn't work like that? Maybe she was dead, but insane, if that was possible.

"That doesn't actually make any damn sense," he finally responded. Sensing that his voice was rising along with his anger, he looked around quickly to see if anyone had noticed, only to realise, of course, that no one other than this woman knew he was there. Everyone else was still blissfully ignoring them.

"Well don't take it out on me," protested Marge, starting to get a bit peeved at his annoying tone. "I don't make the rules. Join a union. Lodge a complaint. I don't care. I'm just tellin' you what Nettie and the others told me when I arrived. Besides, as far as I can see, things back in WhereverWeWere didn't make much sense either. I got two words for you: 'Donald Trump'. What the f*** was that all about? Did that make sense?

"Not to mention the whole damn system. Look, you get born, then you grow up and become a young woman, and you don't know anythin' about how the world works, so you stuff things up for a while. You make some mistakes, hopefully not too big, though some of my friends, I gotta tell you, they made some huge ones, then you get older, until eventually you begin to get the whole thing figured out, only it's too late then, cause you're old, and all your opportunities have passed you by, and then, just when you're *really* startin' to get the hang of it, you die. You think that makes any more sense than this? Cause I don't!"

Wow, thought Peter. *I must have really pushed some of her buttons there.* He decided to try a change of tack.

"Okay. So, what was that you said? 'Unless you get a job'. What's that about?"

"Well, you got two choices here. The first is: you wander around the place, doin' this and that, scarin' some people if that floats your boat, or just keepin' an eye on your grandkids, like I'm doin', and eventually, you get the word you're goin' on, and then you leave. Which is fine, 'specially if you're dressed right, like me. This place'll chill you to the bone. But I passed on in winter, so I got my winter coat with me. You die in summer, like you just did, then likely as not you're gonna be needin' somethin' warmer than what you come here with. Only, what you come here with is all you got. You can't get a change of clothes here like you could back in WhereverWeWere.

"So then there's option two. You get a job. You find a place that's lookin' for a resident spirit — some people call us ghosts, but we prefer 'spirits' — and you see if they got a vacancy. 'Cause, you can't just go into *any* house. You'd bring that chill with you, and cold breezes, and then, on the full moon, they're likely as not gunna see you, and then you're scarin' the shit out of them and all hell's breakin' loose. That's no good for anyone. *And* it's against the rules.

"But, like I say, some places, they got resident spirits. You get a job there and you can stay there. Then you got a warm place to be while you're waitin' to go on. Only catch is, once you take a job like that, you can't leave that place again, even if you try. You're stuck there. It's part of the deal they made with WhereverWeAreGoing. But, like I said, it's warm, and, from everythin' I hear, those jobs are pretty interestin'. Lots of people-watchin' — mainly tourists, of course, 'cause I'm talkin' about places like Olveston, that sort of place.

"And you're allowed to scare the bejesus out of them there. Not too much, mind you. You get too carried away and lose it, like some spirits do, and they'll get one of them exorcists in. You don't want that to happen. You do that and you'll end up WhereNoOneEverWantsToGo before you know what hit you. No. You just do enough to keep yourself from gettin' bored and you'll be fine. Not a bad way to pass the time while you're waitin', hey?"

"Mmm. Maybe. But these rules you mentioned, who decides that? Who sets the rules?"

"Look, I don't know everythin'. Don't claim too, either. I just know they're the rules. Maybe God sets them, maybe the angels, maybe the Great Badger in the Sky, I don't know. They're the rules. That's all I know."

"Fair enough. But what about you? I'm assuming, given that you're down here on the street, that you haven't taken a job."

"That's right. I'm waitin' for my grandkids. They're inside with my daughter. As to why I didn't take a job? Three reasons.

"First, you gotta wait for a vacancy. That don't happen 'til the resident spirit gets the word they're about to move on.

"The second reason is: you gotta get picked for the job. Those jobs are pretty popular, so you gotta get through an interview. And I hate interviews. Hated 'em back in WhereverWeWere and ain't gonna go through any here.

"The third reason is the big one for me, though. I don't want to be stuck in one house. I want to see my grandkids. Want to keep an eye on 'em for as long as I still can. Can't do that if I take a job."

"That makes sense. So, how do I find out about these jobs. Because I'm colder than a shorn sheep right now, and

I haven't got any family here. Sounds like a job might be the best option for me."

"Well, they don't come up often, but, so happens, I've heard there are two goin' right now. Far as I know, you're the first newbie to come along for a while, so you shouldn't have too much competition.

"The first one's just up the hill — at Olveston, actually. Heard just yesterday, Terry's got his marchin' orders. He'll be the one doin' the interviews, by the way. The resident can't go until they pick their replacement.

"The second one's over the other side of the harbour — at Larnach Castle. You can get a bus over there, you know. I don't know whether you figured that out yet or not, but we can ride buses, or go in cars, if there's room. Can't drive 'em, of course. Anyway, not sure whether you'll want that one. It's only part-time."

"Part-time? They've got a job for a part-time ghost, sorry, 'spirit'. I suppose they offer holiday pay too?"

"No need to get smart with me. I'm just tellin' you what's available. Go and ask one of the others if you don't believe me."

"No. No. I'm sorry. That was rude of me. I apologise. How can it be just a part-time job. I don't get that."

"Well, it's all the talk amongst our lot at the moment! Apparently, the spirit there was goin' along fine until her husband turned up amongst the visitors at Larnach one day with a young floozie on his arm. Knocked the spirit completely for six. Before she could get her shit together, they'd been and gone. Then, straight on top of that, she got the word she's movin' on up. Only, she don't want to go now. So, she struck a deal. She'll stay for another six months, but only on a part-time basis. She wants to spend a few days a week scaring the hell out of the floozie. Seems that the floozie was their neighbour when the spirit was back in WhereverWeWere, so now she's wonderin' if somethin' was goin' on before she passed. Anyway, the long and the short of it is there's a vacancy for a part-timer, with the likelihood of becomin' permanent in six months time."

"But is that allowed? I thought you said there were rules. Why would they let her go part-time? Wouldn't there be lots of gho . . . um, spirits who would want that sort of arrangement."

"Yeh. But apparently she said if she don't get what she wants she won't go on to WhereverWeAreGoing. She'll stay here and she'll go apeshit and scare the hell out of everyone who visits Larnach Castle. You know — a bit of head-spinnin' and green vomit and that sort of stuff. She'll keep doin' that until no-one will want to visit the place anymore. The cruise-ship mob won't like that kind of shit."

"Wow. Head-spinning. Can we really do that sort of thing."

"Sure. Takes a bit of practice though. It's bit like ice-skating. You look damned silly 'till you get the hang of it."

"Far out. I got to tell you. There's a hell of a lot to take in about all of this. Anyway, sounds like she's got them over a barrel."

"Yeh."

"Okay. So, I don't think that one's for me. I think I'll go on up to Olveston and see if I can get that job. That sounds more like something I could do. Thank you so much. You've been a huge help. Hope everything goes well for you and your grandkids."

"You're welcome. Good luck. Maybe I'll see you again in WhereverWeAreGoing."

"Sure. Maybe. Bye."

With that, Peter turned and headed back up the hill to Olveston House, all the while wondering at the strange turn his life . . . no . . . his existence, he thought that was probably a better term for his current state . . . wondering at the strange turn his existence had taken. Just a few hours earlier, he'd woken up to what he'd thought was going to be a normal day, only to find that he was . . . well . . . he was 'dead'. It felt weird knowing that word applied to him now. But there it was. He was dead and he just had to make the best of his new life . . . um, existence. Who'd have thought he'd be heading off for an interview for a job as 'The Ghost of Olveston'. It'd be hilarious if it wasn't actually quite serious.

After all, what other options did he have? Either spend what could be months, maybe even years if he was really unlucky, freezing his nuts off wandering the streets of

Dunedin, or take that job over at Larnach Castle, time-sharing with some enraged woman who seemed hell-bent on putting her ex-husband's girlfriend in the loony bin. Nope. Olveston sounded like a pretty sweet deal compared to those options.

It was with these thoughts going through his head that Peter Maynard soon found himself seated in the beautiful old Jacobean building that Dunedin knew as Olveston House.

I *wonder if being bound to the house means literally the house*, he thought, as he looked out through the window at the immaculately tended croquet lawn beyond, *or will I be able to spend some time outside in the lovely gardens. Maybe I'll just be bound to the property. That would be good if that was the case.*

"So, Mr. Maynard. Shall we start." Terry, the resident 'spirit' — like Marge, he had shown an instant disdain for the term 'ghost' — was anxious to get started. Now that a spot was ready for him, he was obviously keen to get to WhereverWeAreGoing. "Can we start with your full name please?"

"Um . . . Peter . . . Peter Alexander Maynard." It wasn't the sort of question Peter had been expecting. What did it matter what his name was?

"Age?"

"Um . . . Sixty-two. Does that matter? Why do you want to know how old I am . . . I mean, was?"

"I don't set the rules, Peter. Could you just answer the

questions please?"

"Okay. Alright. Go on."

"Last address?"

"What? Look, that's just silly. What's that got to do with anything?"

"Do you want this job or not? Or are you going to be one of those difficult ones"

"No. No. Okay. Hart Street, Belleknowes."

"And how long were you a resident of Dunedin?"

"All my life. I was born here."

"Good. And what made you choose Olveston? Why do you want to work here?"

"Well, it was that or Larnach Castle, and I certainly don't want . . . I mean . . . um . . . Olveston is . . . it's such a grand house . . . with such a wonderful history. I would feel quite honoured to be able to be its Resident Spirit, even if only for a short time." Peter thought it best to play this with a straight bat. Terry seemed to take his job very seriously. Best to act as if he would as well.

"Verrry good. Any previous experience?"

"In what way? What sort of experience?"

"As a Resident Spirit. Do you have any previous experience?"

"Well . . . no . . . no . . . but I'm sure I'll get the hang of it quickly. I've always been a quick learner. And I'm keen. Did I say that? I'm very keen. I love Olveston House. It would be great honour."

"Right. No previous experience. Well, in that case, you'll have to take a short practical."

"A what?"

"A practical exam. You'll have to show me that you actually know *how* to be a Resident Spirit. Most of it's pretty self-explanatory. But you *do* have to know how to give the occasional person a scare. That's mandatory I'm afraid."

"Oh. Alright. I'm sure I can do that. What do you want me to do?"

"Well . . . let's see . . . there are one or two visitors in the House at the moment . . . there's a young woman with her daughter . . . no . . . no, I don't think so . . . and then there's that clergyman . . . yes . . . the clergyman. He'll do nicely. I think I saw him go upstairs just before we began. What I want you to do is to go up there and give him a bit of a fright. That should do it. I'll follow you up there and then I'll hang back and watch. Everything else is fine. Give him a good fright and the job is yours."

"Fair enough. I can do that."

Give him a fright? How the hell am I supposed to do that, thought Peter as he wound his way through the house and up the stairs. *Perhaps, if I just creep up behind him, let him feel the cold air as I get up close, and then, all of a sudden, shove my hand right through his back from behind, put it right through to where his heart is. He won't actually feel my skin against his, but I reckon if that doesn't send a quick chill right down to his core, nothing will.* Peter had noticed people give a bit of a shudder as they walked through him earlier on. The clergyman should get the same sort of feeling. That would scare the pants off anyone.

Having reached the top of the landing, he quickly spotted the man he was seeking. The clergyman was standing in a corner, with his back to Peter and Terry. He appeared to be looking at a book he had taken down from the bookshelf he was facing. *Perfect*, thought Peter. *Absolutely perfect.*

He started to slowly creep up to the man, realising too late how much of an amateur he was showing himself to be. Creeping along was totally superfluous; he couldn't possibly be heard. Still, it seemed the right way to go about it, so he stuck with it. Then, all of a sudden, as he moved within reach, he enacted his plan. In a flash he reached out and plunged his hand through the man's back, closing his fist around the spot where his heart should be and giving a shout for added, though probably again, quite superfluous, effect.

"Oh, bugger off," the priest exclaimed, turning to look at where Peter stood, though clearly not able to actually see him. "I'm trying to read here."

Damn, thought Peter despondently as he made his way back down to George Street some five minutes or so later, *this is going to be much harder than I thought. I wonder what time the Number 18 Bus leaves for Larnach. Maybe I'll have time for bit more practice before it goes.*

MARK MCCABE

THE CHAMBER OF THE KRELL

Gazing up at the intricately carved, bas-relief sculpture, Arvid couldn't help but marvel at the skill of the craftsmen who created it, whoever they were. That it was one of the most exquisite pieces of work which had ever been crafted he was in no doubt. But there was something else about it as well, something beyond its sublime elegance, beyond even the enigma of its very existence, something that drew you in to the scene it depicted, as a rabbit is drawn to a baited snare.

It was best not to stare at the images of the island and the sea which surrounded it, the archivist had found. Though they had been carved into the surface of a slab of white marble, if he stared at them long enough, he had found that they began to change. And, once started, the transformation couldn't be stopped. Not until the veil of the static portrait completely dissolved, and the vitality of the living tableau cunningly hidden beneath was revealed in all of its stunning glory. It was a disturbing notion, and one that he couldn't easily dispel.

Arvid had made no mention of these thoughts to the others, of course. It would serve no purpose. He knew it was real just as he knew that the scene itself was an actual place, that it existed somewhere, and not just in the mind of the gifted stonemason who had rendered it. He couldn't explain how he knew that, even to himself, but he'd never felt more certain of anything in his life. After weeks of close inspection, he only had to look at the sculpture now to feel the bond that had grown between him and its subject.

He could feel it happening to him again now. Far from fighting it, however, he welcomed it, just as an addict welcomes the intoxicating fumes of the poppy as he inhales deeply, drawing them in to his body as far as he possibly can. Korman's question could wait.

It was if the scene before him was poised, holding its breath. As soon as he and his colleagues left for the day, heading back up the stairs in a quest for something more wholesome than the dank and musty confines of the chamber, it would slip back into motion. The sea surrounding the rocky outcrop would rise and fall in tandem with the swell of the ocean. A gentle breeze would pick up and the moon would recommence its slow path across an otherwise empty sky, trailing its silvery mantle along the gleaming sands in its wake. Then, in the morning, as soon as he and his fellows returned to the chamber, all motion would stop. A veil of tranquility would settle over the becalmed sea and the whole panorama would be frozen in time once more.

Even now, immobile as it was, the sculpture seemed to pulse with constrained energy. The surf, which had been caught just at that moment when, having retreated as far as it could, it was about to reverse its direction and commence yet another inexorable surge up the moon-drenched shoreline towards the small island's high-water mark, seemed to be chafing at hidden bonds. Arvid could feel the tension, as clearly as he could smell the musty air of the chamber. As he closed his eyes, the image was still fixed in his mind, only the pale gleam of the marble had been replaced by the rich turquoise of deep water, slowly softening as it neared the shore, until it dissipated completely, losing all of its colour in the broiling froth along its leading edge as it surged back up the steep, sandy beach. Taking a deep breath, he gave his other senses full rein, suppressing the stale smell of the long-disused chamber and savouring instead the briny aroma released by the wave as it changed course yet again and slid with increasing speed back down the glistening strand.

The moon, Sythos, if he was not mistaken, for the smaller form of Kaythos was nowhere to be seen, cast its silvery glow over the whole display. By some trick of the craftsman's art, the island's solitary building, a squat tower, tapering slightly as it rose and built of large stone blocks set with thin but clearly discernible lines of mortar, seemed to glisten on the side closest the silvery orb, while its far side lay hidden in shadow.

Not a tree, nor shrub, nor single piece of vegetation could be seen. The only other feature, a small jetty which extended out into the sea from beside the tower, seemed to be waiting, expectantly, for a sail to come up over the horizon, first sign of a craft bound for safe anchorage at its furthest end, beyond the breaking of the incessant waves.

The real jewel, however, the most enigmatic part of the whole tableau, though Arvid couldn't really explain why he felt that to be so, was the solitary door at the foot of the tower. It was closed, but somehow still seemed to speak of wonders that lay hidden behind its wooden surface. For wooden it clearly was, even though it had been carved into the marble. The grain of the oak beams which made up its frame could be seen quite plainly, along with two metal bands and a simple metal handle, about as long as a man's hand and slightly curved upwards at one end. Even a small keyhole, which sat just below the handle, could be seen quite plainly. Arvid resisted the urge to bend down one more time to check if anything was visible through that tiny opening. It was, after all, just a stone carving.

There was no doubt about it, he thought, pulling his thoughts back from where they had drifted, the sculpture was exquisitely done. Its meaning, however, was as enigmatic as the identity of the people who had crafted it. In fact, everything about it was puzzling.

The chamber in which it stood, the Chamber of the Krell if the text was to be believed, had itself lay hidden beneath Tiriana's high citadel for what must have been centuries, possibly even longer. Long forgotten, its chance discovery by an inquisitive labourer while replacing a cracked flagstone had caused quite a sensation amongst the members of the royal court. Then, just as its secrets were being revealed, a long-forgotten scroll had inexplicably fallen from its resting spot high on a shelf in the citadel's library, right at the feet of one of the apprenticed chroniclers.

The scroll, it now seemed, may be as old as the chamber. Not in its current state, of course, but there was reason to believe that the original, of which this one would be simply yet another copy, may go back aeons. It spoke of King Petar, one of Ytain's earliest rulers, and purported to record events which occurred during his reign as if they were contemporaneous. If that was true, then it must have been copied more than a dozen times since that date. More importantly, it also referred to the sculpture, and recorded how King Petar oversaw its installation to both honour and record the 'Pledge of the Krell'.

Which is all very fine, thought Arvid, but who in the name of Ishmir were the Krell? And more to the point, what was their 'pledge', and why had they made it? And by what amazing coincidence had all of these things come to light now, at such a dark hour, with the kingdom facing the likely prospect of such a complete and utter defeat?

Despite his best endeavours, however, and many long days and sleepless nights, neither he, nor any of the motley collection of scholars, theologians, astronomers, alchemists, and scribes working with him, were any closer now to uncovering the answers than they had been when they had started. That wasn't, however, what the High Seneschal wanted to hear.

"Well?" asked Korman with just a hint of exasperation. "I haven't got all day. The palace is in a state at the moment such as you wouldn't believe ... and so is the King. What is it and how do we get our hand on it? Or is this, as I have always suspected, some sort of elaborate joke on the part of our ancestors."

"I doubt if it was intended as a joke, your Grace," responded Arvid, shaking off the trance the Seneschal's voice had called him back from. "It is far too magnificent to be something as coarse as that. As to what it is ... umm ... well ... it would appear that the Krell made a pledge to King Petar, a promise of aid should Ytain ever face its hour of direst need."

"Yes, yes. I know that already. Get on with it."

"And . . . and in order to avail ourselves of this aid, we must travel to the island that is depicted on the sculpture. The aid is . . . it is locked in the tower you can see that stands upon the island."

In desperation, Arvid was making some of this up. The High Seneschal had made it quite clear when he assigned him to this task that failure was not an option. Although what he had said seemed the only likely explanation, they had, in fact, found nothing to confirm what he had just said. The text *did* indicate that the Krell had made such a pledge. It also indicated that King Petar had ordered the sculpture to be created and installed as a record of the pledge. But there was nothing, nothing at all, to indicate just how the sculpture actually connected with the pledge.

"Good. That is good, very good. Well done, Arvid. And what is this aid? What form does it take?"

"It . . . it would appear that it is a . . . a . . . a mighty weapon. We don't know exactly what sort of weapon yet; we're still working on that. But it is a . . . a magical weapon . . . it is a magical instrument of great power. That much we do know."

Arvid clasped his hands behind his back as he finished speaking. He knew that they would be trembling, and he dare not let Korman see that. He also tried to ignore the slow trickle of sweat running down his back, praying that there were no other outward signs of the state of his distress. Everything he had said about the weapon, right down to the revelation that the aid took such a form, was a complete and utter fabrication, a lie. They simply had found nothing to indicate what the Krell's 'aid' actually might be.

"Powerful enough to turn back an army?"

"We don't know, your Grace. A magical weapon of great power. That's all we can say at this point."

"Well, that is progress at least. And how do we get it? How do we get to the island?"

"We haven't been able to uncover that yet, your Grace. We do know that none of our merchants, or fishermen, or sailors of any kind know of an island such as the one depicted in the sculpture. It must be a very long way away from here."

"Mmmmm. Well, keep working on that. Fat lot of good a great weapon will be if we have no idea where to look for it or how to get there."

"Yes, your Grace."

"And what of the Krell? Who are they?"

"They must have died out a long time ago, your Grace. No one has ever heard of them. That may not be important, however. If they left a mighty weapon to aid us in our hour of need, all that is important is where it is and whether it is still where they put it. It seems that they concealed it in the tower on the island. Hopefully, it is still there."

"Indeed. Well, you better get back to it then. Find out where that island is, and quickly. If it takes too much longer, it won't matter anymore. At the rate the Thallosians are progressing, I'm not sure we'll have sufficient time left to go off on some hunt for this thing. Get to it man."

"Yes, your Grace."

Arvid bowed as low as he could and stayed that way until he heard the door shut behind the Seneschal.

"Perhaps if we try tapping it again," he suggested to the workmen awaiting his instructions, once Korman had gone. "Perhaps there is something hidden behind the sculpture itself.

"Be careful, mind you," he called out with some alarm as he saw one of the men bend down to pick up a rather large and foreboding hammer. "I said 'tap', not bludgeon. Whatever else this might be, it is also a work of art. I don't want to be recorded in the next scroll as the man responsible for its destruction."

Having worked late into the evening, Arvid and his team eventually called an end to their labours for the day.

"A fresh start tomorrow will also give us a fresh perspective on this riddle as well," he assured his men as they trudged up the stairs, every one of them eager for a hearty meal and a warm bed.

Early the next morning, before dawn as was their custom,

and after a wholesome breakfast in the citadel's kitchen, the team dutifully made their way back down to the chamber. For the first time since their work had begun, however, Arvid was not there waiting for them. They had become accustomed to the fact that he was always first to arrive and last to leave. But not on this day. He was nowhere to be seen.

A quick run by one of the men up to their quarters to shake him from his slumbers also proved fruitless. He was not still abed either. In fact, no sign of him could be found anywhere in the keep.

It was then that Joryn noticed the pool of water that lay on the floor of the chamber, right at the foot of the wall which held the enigmatic carving that had defied all attempts to decode its meaning.

"This wasn't here yesterday," exclaimed Joryn when he accidentally stepped in the puddle. "Where could this have come from? Did one of you spill something here?"

"That's far too much water for a spill," replied one of the other men. "There must be several buckets of the stuff." Squatting down as he spoke, the man dipped a finger into the liquid and brought it up to his tongue.

"Damn! It's salty. If I didn't know any better, I'd say this is sea water. Why would anyone bring several bucketloads of sea water down here and empty them across the floor, right beneath the carving. Maybe Arvid stayed up late conducting some strange experiment last night."

"But look," cried another. "The puddle is directly beneath

the part of the sculpture that depicts the beach and those incoming waves."

At that, all eyes lifted to the sculpture.

"By the gods," gasped another of the men in a trembling voice. "The tower. Look at the tower. The door on it. It's open. It's open. That can't be. It wasn't open. It was closed. That can't be. It's not . . . "

As he spoke all eyes turned as one to look at the tower. And in that instant a cacophony of cries of despair, gasps, and strangled groans rose up from the team of men. For as they watched, transfixed by the horror of what was unfolding before them, a small, black-sleeved arm reached out through the open door on the rock carving, took a hold of the handle and slowly pulled it closed.

At the very instant of its closing, cries of alarm and pandemonium rang out from the stairway leading down from the hall above the chamber. Above the cries, the sound of a bell could be heard, incessantly ringing out the alarm. The citadel was under attack.

The invading army had force-marched through the night under the cover of darkness, somehow covering an impossible distance in the time available to them while at the same time evading detection by any of the innumerable scouts that had been posted to prevent such an eventuality. The dawn had been its signal to attack, and it was now approaching the walls. Every defender available was being called to arms. Ytain's fate was about to be decided.

Whatever hope there had been of aid was gone, as suddenly and unexpectedly as Arvid's disappearance, though none, at the time, saw a connection between the two events.

About the Author

Mark McCabe had an extensive career in senior executive positions in the Australian public sector before retiring from his position as the Australian Capital Territory's Work Safety Commissioner in 2016.

Mark holds a BA majoring in English and Latin from the Australian National University and a Diploma in Editing and Proofreading from the New Zealand Institute of Business Studies.

Since his retirement from formal work, as well as publishing several fantasy novels, Mark has established an editing and publishing business in northern New South Wales, Australia.

Serotine Editing and Publishing Services offers a range of publishing and editing services with a particular focus on helping indie authors get their work published and available in the marketplace.

ALSO BY THE AUTHOR

Fiction

Between the Hammer and the Anvil

As Fire is to Gold

When All the Leaves Have Fallen

As Fire is to Gold: The Complete Chronicles of the
Ilaroi

Non- Fiction

Self-Publishing: A Step-By-Step Guide